Holly Day's *Café*
and Other Christmas Stories

Holly Day's
Café
and Other
Christmas Stories

Gerald R. Toner

PELICAN PUBLISHING COMPANY

Gretna 1996

Copyright © 1996
By Gerald R. Toner

*The word "Pelican" and the depiction of a pelican are trademarks
of Pelican Publishing Company, Inc., and are registered
in the U.S. Patent and Trademark Office.*

Library of Congress Cataloging-in-Publication Data

Toner, Gerald R.
    Holly Day's Café and other Christmas stories/Gerald R. Toner.
        p.   cm.
    ISBN   1-56554-204-5 (hc : alk. paper)
    1. Christmas stories, American.   I. Title.
    PS3570.0484H6   1996
    813'.54–dc20   96-12086
                                                              CIP

Manufactured in the United States of America

Published by Pelican Publishing Company, Inc.
1101 Monroe Street, Gretna, Louisiana 70053

Contents

CHAPTER 1

The Snow

"IT'S TIME TO CLOSE UP." Maggie Day undid her apron, tossed it on the counter, and stretched her back. She was bending with age but not bent, testing sixty but not there yet.

"You don't have to make it sound so final!" Will Joseph laughed, but he didn't argue. He never argued with the boss, and Maggie was still the boss.

"It is final. Now clean up and get on home." Her cranky staccato punctuated each word like a familiar song. Will's lanky frame slumped even as Maggie straightened up. There was no arguing with her. He had tried that over the past few weeks and failed.

"Look, Miss Day, it's already Christmas Eve!" Will's pronouncement made Maggie jump. She turned. Will was pointing to the old wall clock above the cash register. The hands were barely visible through the yellow film of cooking grease.

"So it is," Maggie nodded, "but you don't have to shout it and you don't have to call me Miss Day!"

"I've always called you Miss . . ."

"Nineteen years is a short 'always,' Will. You'll know what I mean in another forty years. Until then call me Maggie."

"I don't know, Miss Day . . ."

"Maggie," she interrupted.

"I mean, that would feel funny."

"Not as funny as having a grown man treating me like his invalid grandma! Now call me Maggie or you're fired!"

"Okay," he faltered, "Maggie." Will moved at his tasks faster than ever, embarrassed as always by Maggie's bluntness. Maggie shook her head. He was so young. So good. He had a lot of mistakes to make if he was going to enjoy life.

"When are the video people taking over?" he asked.

"Hmm?" For a moment she forgot her fiction about the buyers from Nashville. "Oh yeah, them. Well, soon enough. Soon enough."

Will passed the old wood stove and gave it a friendly kick. "You never did get it fixed."

"You're right. I didn't." She picked up their coffee cups from early in the evening and shoved them through the counter window.

"And now it's too late," his voice sank.

Her voice assumed an unfamiliar edge. "And why should I throw good money after bad?" She paused, thinking to herself, then adding quietly, "Besides, they're dangerous. You can burn a place down with one of those. Sure enough."

"Not if you watch 'em."

"Will, why don't you just argue about it?" Almost forty years separated Will and Maggie, but they acted at times like sparring lovers.

Will retreated to his nightly routine of turning the chairs up on the table, getting out the broom, and sweeping up the trash. When he was finished he would clean out any dirty ash trays and wipe off the table tops. He did his work quickly and in silence. Maggie hummed some old tune from the fifties.

Will started drawing the old, tattered pull shades on the front bank of windows. She watched him. Will moved as if all life was ahead—fast, clipped, not a hint of weariness even though it was past midnight. He deserved more than life was liable to give him: college, a little savings to start out, a car, some new clothes, the right girl. Maggie would do what she could.

Will stopped before he pulled the last shade. "We're going to get snow for Christmas."

Maggie hooted. "Not likely."

"Look at those clouds. Those are big old snow clouds. All puffed up pink and purple!"

"That's the street light reflecting!" she huffed.

"Well, I know that. But all the same, it's going to snow."

"Get your coat, Will. Time to lock up."

Will kept staring at Maggie as he slipped into his football jacket.

He pulled the brim of his baseball cap down on his forehead and grinned.

"It's going to snow."

"Go home, Will."

"I'll be back tomorrow," he shouted as he threw open the door.

"I'm closing, Will! Closing!" she called after him. The wind howled, the door slammed, and she was alone.

Maggie wandered back to the window. Will had left the shade up, almost as if he wanted to remind her of his prediction. Snow. She gazed at the low, thick clouds. It never snowed at Christmas in Christian. Not for thirty years or more at least. And not this Christmas for sure! Cold and rain, yes, but not snow.

She turned from the window and looked around her. Almost sixty years of memories tied up in one place. The only place she could remember as a child. The only place she had ever called home. The only thing she had of any worth—and it wasn't worth much.

She walked in a slow circle around the small dining room, rimmed with booths on two sides and counter and stools on the other two. The red vinyl upholstery was crisscrossed with duct tape. The chrome on the chairs was rusted at the bottoms. Not much value in them. There were pictures on the walls, but not many. A photo of the place from the forties—back when her mother and father had started it. A yellowed clipping from the *Louisville Courier-Journal*: "Vaudevillians Make Home Away From Home for the Boys." There was a juke box that didn't work too well and a wood stove that didn't work at all and a cash register that worked just fine on the rare occasions when it got some use. What was the term her insurance policy used for the worth of all this stuff? "Actual cash value."

When she got to the counter she reached over it, groping along the shelf beneath for her special reserve Maker's Mark. She filled the bottom of a clean coffee cup and sat down in her rocker. For a while, before she went to the back room and bed, she would rock and sip and get sleepy. She tightened her sweater around her scrawny shoulders and stared out the window. Will was right. It did look like snow. It felt like snow too; the damp, cold that got between her shoulder blades and made her back ache. The weather was going to change. That was for sure. But snow? She shook her head. The mind was like a clever pet; it knew how to play up to you, telling you things just because it knew you wanted to believe, not because it was true. She wanted snow. She wanted something, anything to be different on the day after closing. Maggie clinched her fingers around the ends of the rocker arms. It wasn't fair. The anger she'd suppressed for Will suddenly gushed out. It wasn't fair. Not the café closing. Not all that was past. Not life. She gritted her teeth and sipped again. She'd show 'em. She'd show 'em all.

As the bourbon warmed her and the soft hue of reflected light filled her café, Maggie's thoughts tumbled into each other and her anger subsided. The past rushed at her like some semi. She didn't think of the past very often. But Christmas could do that to you if you didn't watch it. The mere thought of it sent her memories racing. Not that she wanted to think of the past. The sweet times were too long ago. The café was closing. The café was all that she'd ever known.

Maggie slapped her palms on the arm of the chair. If she didn't watch it, the Maker's would have her crying next. The old familiar routine. First she mellowed, then she felt sorry for herself, then she teared up, then she went to bed. But not tonight, she told herself. Tonight thoughts of the past catapulted her into thoughts of the future—the immediate future. After all those years, after those thousands of gallons of coffee and tons of steak and eggs, what did she have? A café and an acre of land. That and two insurance policies—one on her and one on the café. It would be a shame to let the one on the café go to waste. She wasn't sure about the other.

Maggie rocked and rocked. Her eyes fluttered and her breathing deepened. Time to go to bed. Tomorrow would give her more time to think and to act, if that's what she decided to do. She stood up, stretched, then went to the window and started to pull down the shade. The clouds were dense, thickening by the minute. Maybe there was something in Will's prediction. It sure looked like snow—and a lot of it. But then it never snowed like that at Christmas. She left the shade untouched and shuffled off to the back bedroom.

❄ ❄ ❄ ❄ ❄ ❄ ❄ ❄ ❄ ❄

The old Big Ben clanged inches from her face. Maggie stirred, trying to awaken. Her fumbling fingers silenced it. Peace. She had been dreaming. In her dreams, crowds of customers were yelling back and forth to each other. One of them was urging her to do something. She couldn't make out his face but she could hear his laughter. The music was loud, the juke box roaring. Just like the old days. She strained to see who was there. Did she know them? Were they friends? There was a rich smell that thickened the air.

The aroma of people living closely to their desires. The alarm interrupted and her dreams ended.

Her eyelids fluttered. Time to get up. Time to do her job. She stopped just as she was about to throw the comforter back. What job? Holly Day's was closed. Nobody knew but her and Will, but if anyone did show up, she'd tell them, "She's closed." She'd say it with a tight grin and an edge in her voice. "I'll give you a cup of coffee, but it's on the house. She's closed." She wondered, half asleep, whether she would be able to do it. At the end of the day there would be other decisions to make. Other plans to carry out. Holly Day's in a blaze of glory! She opened one eye through a cloud of sleep dew, squinting at the clock face.

"Oh no!" she groaned. It was 7:30 A.M.. Work day or not, she'd overslept again. "Will!" she cried out. "Will Joseph!" she repeated. He'd said he'd be back.

Will had become her crutch in the morning as well as the evening. For five years he had opened up Holly Day's just after six in the morning, headed up the road for school around eight, and returned after football or basketball practice for the dinner trade. He had done his homework at her counter and he had sipped coffee with her in the evenings. Since graduation he had worked full time—going on two years—to make money for college. He'd spent a lot of time at Holly Day's. Too much time maybe. But she never told him that. She didn't dare, for fear that he might agree.

"Will," she called one last time. No answer. Only an eerie silence. It wasn't like Will to be late. She felt a chill across her shoulders. Maybe the boy had had an accident in the dark. Run down by some speeding drunk. Or beaten up out on the main drag. The local morons were always ready to bash somebody. It was easier than work. A dozen scenarios raced through her mind.

Maggie threw back the covers and sat up. For a second the heat from the old down comforter stayed with her and obscured the cold—but only for a second. The temperature had dropped twenty degrees since midnight. The short hairs on her neck stood up and her arms began to shake. She reached down to the foot of her bed and pulled her mother's crazy quilt around her like the train of an eccentric queen.

Maggie stood up. Her bare feet made contact with the cold linoleum and she did an arthritic jig. She flopped back down, leaned over, and groped under the bed for her slippers. She searched around for a second, then found them.

In the old days she had opened the place by herself. She was up, dressed, and on the floor before the short-order cooks, the counter waitresses, and the check-out clerk. She made the first, best pot of coffee in the morning and she usually made the last one past midnight most nights. Late to bed. Early to rise. No matter how early, she had been ready for the day. Five A.M. Six A.M. Whatever the traffic demanded. The lights of Holly Day's Café would flash on in the predawn chill and stay on after the Sunoco station down the street was dark as a graveyard. Those were the days when they filled the joint in search of the best coffee and the freshest pie for a hundred-mile stretch of U.S. 31W.

"Good riddance!" Maggie answered her own daydreams. Those times were ancient history. Gone with the coming of the expressway. Twenty, no thirty years before. She wondered how Holly Day's had lasted this long.

Maggie fumbled for her slippers, stood up again, and drew a breath. The air rushing into her lungs was cold and refreshing, like an icy sherbet. Maggie smiled. Quitting the cigarettes two years before had helped. She missed them, but it sure felt good breathing without them. She thought of the young doctor who had charmed her into breaking the habit. Like everyone else in Christian worth a damn, he'd moved on.

The exhaust from her lungs shot outward in a cloud. She threw herself into the morning's exercise. Up and down. Up and down. Touch her toes. Up to her waist. Down to her toes again. Twist to the left. Twist to the right. Stretch up and wiggle her fingers. Work out the cold, joint by joint. Maggie froze in a pose of unintended supplication.

"Good thing . . . " Maggie said to herself, still thinking about the demise of the café, ". . . about time." Her disjointed words were part of a never-ending conversation she carried on during the hours when Will wasn't around. Maggie brushed aside thoughts of the café's demise, or her own. When the time came, she'd know what to do. Out in a blaze of glory!

Maggie lowered her arms to her side. Enough exercise! She wasn't sure why Christmas had surprised her this year. Time flew faster the older she got. That was natural enough. But not this fast! It seemed as if Thanksgiving had only been a week or so before. Maybe it was the weather that put her off stride. Until mid-December it had been more like summer than fall. Then wham— an Arctic cold front had dropped into the South and it was all she could do to avoid buying another tank of LP gas.

Maggie caught her breath and slipped on her old, loose-fitting khakis, cotton turtleneck, and chunky wool sweater. She started for the door to the restaurant, then stopped long enough to brush her hair and put on a little makeup.

Time to clean up and wind down. The day would pass without fanfare or requiem. No farewell from the appreciative customers, no sign-off from WCHR. For a moment it made her blue, then she forced a laugh. No time for self-pity. Not for Maggie Day.

She threw open the back door of the restaurant and made her entrance, an actress playing to an empty house. Not that she was expecting anyone—unless it was Lanny or Buddy or Will, arriving late. What she saw instead made her gasp.

"Whoa, God 'a mercy!'"

Through the window left uncovered the night before Maggie saw that the world had changed. It was no longer awash in blacks and grays, but only white. The snow Will had predicted had arrived, only it wasn't just a powdery dusting or a wet blanket that would melt by noon. This was a blizzard, layering the countryside like whipped cream. And the snow was still falling. Maggie stood in awe. For an instant she felt like she might cry. Then she caught herself with a grunt and started lifting the shades until the dining room was awash in the snow's reflected light.

She stared out at what had been Main Street. Bright, blinding crystals were piled up in drifts outside the windows on the porch. John's Corner Grocery had disappeared beneath a thick blanket of white and there wasn't a storefront within a hundred yards that looked anything like it had the night before. The electrical and phone lines hung down with ice and the trees looked like snowmen. There were no cars, no traffic. Oh, it's beautiful, she thought, like a Christmas card or a child's fantasy.

Maggie's lips squeezed tight. Beautiful and deadly. It was still snowing. Her fears for Will returned. If the bad roads hadn't gotten him the night before, maybe they had gotten him this morning. There had never been a blizzard like this in Christian. Not in her memory. Storms had shut down the schools and even closed the businesses for a day, but those storms were in January or February and they never looked like this one. This one had silenced everything. Storms like this stopped traffic and broke power lines and even killed people. A thought flitted across her consciousness—if Holly Day's had a fire on a day like this, there'd be no way the volunteers could get there in time.

Maggie shook her head and the idea passed. Will was out there somewhere. First thing was to see him safe and sound. "Make the coffee," she muttered to herself.

She started measuring out the Maxwell House, filling the pots with clear cold water, flipping on the automatic drip. She went back to the little kitchen and fired up the grill. If the regulars did make it in, she would show them she was ready. Ready for food, a cup of coffee, the latest gossip—even if she was closed. She was ready for anything except loneliness.

She knew the loneliness. It struck like a hungry wolf separated from its pack. It demanded to be fed, to be nurtured, to be cared for even if it only promised to eat her up by way of gratitude. Maggie shivered, clutching her arms tightly about herself. So this was how the last day would end—alone. Will wouldn't even make it. She would have no one to talk to, to jab in the ribs, to bump with her hip. She wanted the loneliness to be gone, to skulk back out the door and let her be. But she knew it wouldn't oblige. The coffee started to bubble and gurgle. Maggie turned on the ancient Philco over the counter window. Its tubes warmed and crackling static turned to music.

"I'm dreaming of a white Christmas," the old crooner sang, "just like the ones I used to know . . ."

"I never knew one like this, Bingo!" She turned the radio up and made Mr. Crosby her companion. ". . . where the tree tops glisten," she joined him, "and children listen, to hear sleigh bells in the snow . . ." She interrupted her duet, "Only easy on the snow!"

The smell of fresh coffee invaded Holly Day's. The heat of the grill began to erase the chill. As if nothing had changed! One way or another she would survive the old café's demise. She was afraid. Afraid of a lot of things. But she would make this Christmas Eve a good one, by God.

CHAPTER 2

Traveling North

LEO DEANGELIS POURED ANOTHER CUP of coffee from his thermos. The smell of the hot black brew was the only friendly sign he could conjure. The cup was warm, his hands icy cold. The roads were getting worse. Rain had turned to snow at the Alabama-Tennessee border. In Minnesota or South Dakota or upper New York state they would know what to do with snow like this. The plows would come through like a tank division and the convoys would roll along. Not here. They didn't know what to do with it. So the roads had gone from bad to worse and then to impossible.

A driver with any sense would pull off and wait it out. But Leo was going to keep going. He had a load of fresh fruit and it would rot if he let it sit for a day. Not that anyone would blame him for it. He had been at it long enough that no one would question his judgment. Better to stop than risk losing the load. Leo smiled and turned up the radio. Sense, hell. He was going to keep going. Keep going till they closed the roads.

He fiddled with the dials. Even the country stations were playing Christmas songs. Good reason, being the day before Christmas. The word itself was enough to send his mind spinning. Christmas meant family, going home, sitting in front of a fire, and taking the day easy. "I'm dreaming of a white Christmas . . ." the voice crackled. Fifty years old and still they played that recording.

Every time he thought he had it licked, the memories came rolling back on him like some head wind. Then he would grit his teeth to hold back the tears. They were gone. A wife and two children. Lost to a dark night and a narrow country road, killed the instant the drunk crossed the solid center line. And where had he been? Another Christmas on the road. Two days straight driving brought him back. How many years now? Five, no ten. He couldn't keep it straight. Life was like that on the open road. Life was like that as the years piled up. The tears should have stopped long ago. That's what he told himself. But his heart had never listened to his brain. No dam could stop tears when they wanted to overflow.

Their faces had gotten hazy in his mind's eye. That's why he kept their pictures clipped on the front of the cab. As the years had passed he had begun to feel more like part of their world than his own. His wife's hairdo had become dated. The same with his son's shirt and his daughter's dress. But with time he felt more a part of their world than that of the living.

Sometimes he spoke to them, especially after midnight. He let them know what the day had been like or where he was heading or what job was coming up next. Every once in a while some little adventure turned up on the road and he used them as a sounding board for whether he'd done the right thing. On rare occasions, usually in the hours before dawn, he thought he heard them: "Leo" spoken in his wife's Southern drawl. "Dad" in a girl's voice or "Daddy" in a boy's. When he heard the voices it spooked him. Not enough to stop him from answering, but always enough to make him pull over for more coffee. He was afraid. He'd never admit it, but he was. Afraid he was losing touch with the world. He wasn't quite ready for that. Sometimes he didn't like the world much, but it was all he knew.

❆ ❆ ❆ ❆ ❆ ❆ ❆ ❆ ❆ ❆

Sarah Herald sat on the toilet seat, the bathroom door locked, thick, salty tears pouring over her cheeks, her thin figure heaving with emotion. She had come within a hair of striking Julie. She had never struck her before, except for the spanking she gave her once for sticking a screwdriver into an electrical outlet. Even that brief corporal punishment had left Sarah guilt ridden for a week. But this time it wasn't a spanking, or a time-out, or even a grab on the arm. She had almost smacked her six-year-old daughter across the cheek. That's what had sent her running to the bathroom for a moment's solace. In an instant she had slipped from super mom, assistant dean of students, and head of the house to a refugee from the morning talk show confessionals—"I beat my child and hate myself for it!"

She wondered if it had really been over a choice of coats.

"Julie Herald, you heard me, now *please* get your down jacket with the hood!" Sarah had stared out the bay window at streets and yards covered with six new inches of snow.

"I don't like the hood. I want to wear my green coat with the velvet collar!" Julie held her fists and stomped her right foot.

"Then we're not going up the highway to meet your father."

Julie had paused, weighing her mother's threat. "Daddy will come get me."

Sarah shifted uneasily. Julie was right. Her father would gladly drive to hell and back for his daughter. If he'd felt the same way about her, Sarah thought, she might never have gotten the divorce.

"That's not your father's call. Besides, the snow's got to be worse in Cincinnati. He couldn't get to us and I'm not sure we can get to him—even if you *do* put your down coat on!"

"I'm wearing my pretty coat!" Julie had stated defiantly. They had continued the back and forth argument for a few more minutes before Sarah sensed that she was about to lose control. Then she had retreated to the bathroom.

Sarah wiped her cheeks with a wad of toilet paper. What had upset her so much? Not a silly coat, she thought. Not even the helplessness she felt every time she and Julie disagreed over what to wear, or eat for breakfast, or watch on television. Maybe it was how much Julie reminded her of Sam: hardheaded and stubborn—never yielding, always determined. Maybe Julie got it from her as well. That was what her sister had said the night before on the phone.

"But I'm right and he's wrong!"

"Spoken like a true combatant."

"Are you taking his side?"

"I'm just saying that if the weather is as bad as they say it's going to be, give him a call and tell him you'll be a little late." Her sister was always cool, sensible, the perfect diplomat.

"We've got our schedule and we've got to keep it."

"Now who's being hardheaded? Call him, Sarah. He'll understand. I know he will."

"Whose side are you on?"

"My side! I don't want to visit you and Julie in some hospital on Christmas!"

"Very funny."

Her sister's voice lost its sarcasm, her delivery direct and to the point. "People get killed in storms like this."

"Aren't we cheery this evening!"

"I'm not kidding."

"Do you have to be right *all* of the time?" Sarah conceded.

"That's my role in life, Sarah."

Sarah laughed. That's all she could do. Then she agreed she would call him. They hung up and her resolve faded. She tried once, let the phone ring three times, and hung up before the recorder could engage. Bad weather would hold off a little while longer. She had been sure of it the night before.

Sarah emerged from the bathroom resolved that she would never come close to smacking Julie again. One look out the front bay window and she knew that her sister had been right. A magnolia that had never borne the weight of wet snow now bent to the ground, creaking and groaning with its weight. Cars had become caricatures of themselves, sharp lines softened with what looked like cake icing. There was no street any more.

Sarah's eyes were red and her cheeks looked puffy but she had fixed her makeup and convinced herself that Julie wouldn't notice.

"Why were you crying, Mommy?" Julie was waiting for her.

Sarah stared at Julie and debated whether to lie.

"I was crying . . ." she paused, like a game show contestant trying desperately to fill the blank before the buzzer sounds, ". . . because it's Christmas." The words came out freely and they were true. She wasn't about to explain.

"Christmas is a happy time!" Julie exclaimed.

Sarah laughed. "You watch too many movies."

"You don't believe enough!" Julie's chin raised when she was lecturing someone. Just like her father.

Sarah said nothing. Julie was probably right.

"I'll wear my down coat," Julie capitulated.

Sarah glanced out the window again. "Don't worry about it, pumpkin. I don't think we're going anywhere."

"But we've got to go!"

"Julie, look outside."

Julie complied. "So?"

Sarah had forgotten that Julie had only seen snow on television. She didn't know what it did to the highways.

"Because the roads will be covered up. We'll leave tomorrow . . . or whatever. We'll think of something."

Julie held her breath, trying not to cry. When she let it out, her tears exploded. "You promised."

Sarah kneeled by her daughter's side and offered her arms. It was no consolation. Julie turned and buried her head in the couch. Another empty promise, Sarah thought. The internal debate raged. Should she give in to the wishes of her six-year-old, or give in to common sense and live with failure for the rest of the day? Fulfill her promise, but risk their safety? Exercise her parental rights, but know that once more Sarah Herald just couldn't quite deliver? Her arms dropped to her side in resignation.

"Get your coat on!" Sarah heard her own words and knew that there was no going back.

"We're going! We're going!"

"We're *leaving*, pumpkin. If the weather gets worse or the roads are bad, we're coming back." She tried to save her option to retreat even if she knew it was lost. Once on the road they would plod onward like a grim-faced army. She knew it and Julie knew it.

Julie jumped up and grabbed her down coat. Then she rushed to the door, flopped down, and started slipping on her bright red snow boots. Sarah smiled. Her daughter wasn't going to give her time to change her mind.

Sarah made a pass through the house, turning off lights, locking the back door, and making sure the cat had food. By the time she slipped on her own parka, Julie was standing impatiently by the front door singing Christmas carols to herself. Sarah paused to take it in. Remember these scenes, she told herself. All too soon they'll be gone. Like Christmas itself.

Christmas. There was the standing invitation to stop by her sister's in Louisville. One of the unmarrieds in the president's office had told her to call if she headed up to Indianapolis. (Did he know she was four years older than him?) He would be there with his parents. She could always drive back home and spend Christmas alone—the most likely scenario by far.

"Okay, pumpkin, let's hit the road."

Julie opened the front door and a blast of wind snatched it from her. Sarah rushed to her aid, turning her face from the showering shards of snow and slamming the front door shut. The icy slivers stuck like tiny knives. Even the simple walk to the car seemed like a trek. Sarah shivered, but not from the cold this time. It came from the realization that the car would be cold, the roads slick, and the storm unrelenting.

There was no turning back. Sarah settled Julie in the passenger seat, grabbed the scraper from the glove compartment, and went to work. Her face tingled, her eyes watered. Ten minutes later she had cleared enough spaces to see where she was going. Then she jumped into the car and turned the ignition, half hoping the engine was dead. It clicked, then growled, and finally sputtered into action. If God had wanted her to stay home . . . she rationalized. Wipers on, defroster on. Things were beginning to seem a little more civilized. She looked over at Julie. She was staring straight ahead, her down jacket zippered tight beneath her chin, ready for the adventure to begin. Sarah smiled. So much turmoil over a coat.

"Wait here, I'll be back in a second."

"Forget something?" Julie averted her gaze for only an instant.

"Yes . . . your coat with the velvet collar. Who knows what your dad's got planned for Christmas!"

CHAPTER 3

Will Arrives

MAGGIE'S DUET WITH THE LATE MR. CROSBY ended and she began to fumble with the dials of her AM antique. Time to get some hard news about the weather. The numbers on the front of the Philco had long since worn away but her fingers knew the turn of the dial like it was braille.

"Get a nice little Sony AM/FM with a CD player," Will had urged her the summer before.

"And what am I going to do with a CD player, seeing as how I don't have any CDs?"

"Okay then, just get an FM radio."

"And what business would a cranky old woman like me have listening to some rock station out of Nashville!"

"You're not old!" Will had grinned.

"Well you're right there . . . punk . . ." her best Clint Eastwood, ". . . but just the same . . . I don't need a new radio! And that's final."

Maggie smiled at the memory of her banter with Will. She would miss him. Now that Holly Day's was closing he'd have to go on to college. There wasn't anything else to do! She turned the dial slowly clockwise.

". . . to ten below zero by early evening." The steadfast voice of Christian's own WCHR weatherman was caught in mid-sentence.

"Snow accumulation of up to two feet is expected in the outlying regions."

"What do you mean 'outlying regions,' Orville?" Maggie chided the radio. "The whole county's an outlying region!"

"Local authorities are reporting road conditions impassable and crews have been out since the early morning hours. From the Judyville police post WCHR spoke to Trooper Buddy Wendell."

"Buddy Wendell! On radio! No wonder he missed coffee! I forgive you, Buddy! I forgive you!"

"All roads throughout the western and central portions of the state are extremely hazardous. Travelers are advised to proceed with the greatest caution. All warnings will be in effect throughout the day."

"Tell 'em, Buddy!" Maggie cheered. "Man'll be wanting his own talk show next!" she mumbled. "And now, from Christian, Kentucky, the voice of the people, The Buddy Wendell Show!" she announced to herself.

"In the event of any form of mechanical difficulties motorists are urged to pull off the road to the nearest exit."

"His own gal Friday, a new squad car, maybe even a helicopter." Maggie loved it when Buddy couldn't argue back.

Wendell concluded and the weatherman resumed. A snowstorm was his time to shine. School and plant closings were easy. There were only two of each. The schools were closed for the holidays anyway. He started down a list of grocery stores, gas stations, restaurants: all closed. Maggie's interest died and her thoughts meandered back to Will.

Where's Will? she thought, I need that boy for chores and errands and all kinds of stuff. She needed him for more than his brawn but her grumbling mind denied it. Her eyes began to film up again as she combined the end of Holly Day's with the end of her days with Will. "I want him now!" she finally said out loud.

She didn't hear the door open and the wind gust through the café as Will Joseph entered. He heard her words before the door closed with a bang. Maggie started.

"Who were you talking to, Miss Day?"

"Who do you think?" Maggie's startled retort didn't make any sense, but she said it with such authority that he could only fumble.

"Well, uh, I don't know . . ."

"Where in heaven's name have you been?"

"My car froze up. I've been working on it for almost an hour." He blew on his hands and stamped his boots free from snow. "I finally got a jump and it warmed up—kind of."

"Well I thought I was going to pack up the old place without you!"

"Couldn't we leave it open through the winter?"

"Then the spring and the summer . . . don't start again, Will. It's a done deal. No more Holly Day's. Period. Got me?" Maggie hurried about the room, taking pictures from the wall and laying them on the counter.

"Yeah. Okay. But *if* you could run the place like in the old days . . ."

"Will Joseph, what do you know about the 'old days'? The last old days worth talking about happened before you were born!"

"What about the first Christmas after the war? When you and Holly and your mom and dad were all on NBC?"

Maggie ceased her make-work puttering. "We weren't on NBC. Not exactly. 'Course I was still pretty young. But the old WCHR news man got wind of the fact that we were puttin' up a slew of stranded soldiers on their way home . . . it snowed a bunch that year . . . and I'll be damned if word didn't get around and Bob Hope and Bing Crosby both didn't send those boys a message down here at Holly Day's! We weren't *on* NBC . . . not Mom and Dad . . . but they talked to us over the radio and it felt like we were big time!" Maggie caught herself wiping a tear away, then snapped herself out of the past and started packing up again. "Now Will, I wish you'd stop that!"

"Okay, okay," Will turned red and stammered. "But I bet it was something when you and Holly and your mom and dad ran this place!" He had heard all of her tales before. A dozen times. Sometimes in the evenings after she had had more than a few drinks too many. But he loved them. He craved them, like favorite lines from a movie.

"Yeah, sure." Maggie tried to divert his attention by fussing over the framed photos and newspaper clippings arrayed on the counter.

"Do you ever see the guys in that picture?" Will examined one of the yellowed photos as she skimmed a dust rag over it.

"Are you kidding?" Maggie turned to pour a cup of coffee. "I only saw 'em for a few minutes after the picture was taken!"

"But it must have been fun in the old days."

"I had a lot of fun. Type of fun you should be having." The boy's fascination with the past pleased and bothered her at the same time. Those times in the past had been special. Will knew it and it took a special boy to care like he did. But sometimes he cared too much. Sometimes he lived more in her past than she did.

Will pored over one photo after another. "How come there's none of Holly?" He held his cup in both hands and let the aroma fill his nose.

The mention of Holly's name paralyzed Maggie midway through refilling her cup. "Tell you the truth, Will, Holly hated pictures. Pretty as she was, she wouldn't pose for nothing!"

"Tell me what the place was like when you and Holly ran it." Maggie shook her head and her expression took on the faraway quality Will associated with drink. Her eyes glistened and she seemed to be looking right through him. Then she shook her head as if to awaken.

"Nah, not today. Christmas is too sad for all of that old times stuff!"

"What do you mean, sad? It's Christmas Eve!"

"It can be a pretty blue Christmas if your friends and family are all gone."

"When was this taken?" He urged a picture on her that showed a young Maggie and some soldier under a big clump of mistletoe.

Maggie examined the photo and tried to think back. "Fifty-two, maybe fifty-three. I was a kid."

"You were awful pretty."

"If I weren't so dirt poor, I'd think you were buttering me up for a spot in my will!" She quickly lost herself in the photo. "I had a cute little figure way back then. Tight little rear. Hair over one eye . . . a regular Veronica Lake!" Maggie leaned against the counter, trying to detect if Will understood the allusion. He didn't.

"Who's the soldier?"

"Lord if I know!" Maggie waved her hand. "Seemed like every soldier between Fort Campbell and Fort Knox hit this place at one time or another. Couple of them made Holly their pin-up girl . . . strictly respectable. But she danced better, flirted a lot, and kept the boys in their place easier than I ever did." She re-examined the picture and started picking out details. "This was a hopping joint! Juke box was always going back then. If not, then the piano. See the grill? You could get breakfast any time of day. Bacon, eggs . . ." She paused. "Lord, this place smelled good. Hot apple pie in the afternoon . . . the smell of coffee and fresh cigarettes night and day . . ." Maggie rearranged the bun in her hair, "Come to think of it, the place was a regular health hazard!" Will laughed and Maggie slid back into the present. "What's happening out there?"

"Out there?" Will repeated. "It's bad. Nothing much moving unless it's got four-wheel drive."

"Jasper and Oma okay?" Maggie always asked about Will's foster parents.

"They're keeping warm. Staying inside. Uncle Jasper's refinishing an old pie safe. Aunt Oma's putting together Christmas dinner."

Maggie wondered why he never called them Mom and Dad. Will loved them. She was sure of that, but they were always Aunt Oma and Uncle Jasper.

"Well, we'll be finished in here by noon. Then we'll settle up the week's wages and you can get back to them."

"I'll stay," Will said.

"Like I said, we'll settle up and then I got some personal things to look after."

"Let me buy it, Maggie." He paused. "When you move to Florida, I mean. You could come back and visit and . . ."

"Cut that talk, Will." Her voice showed her irritation. "Your money's paying for school next year."

"I waited one year. I can wait two or three or more."

"You do and you'll never go."

"So?"

"So then you'll be stuck in Christian 'til it blows away! Now that's enough. Your money's saved for school!" She swatted her dish towel at Will. "Understand?"

"I understand, but Holly Day's is special. That's all."

"Will," Maggie reached over and placed her hand on his shoulder. "You're special. My memories are special. People who are dead were special. Some of the folks that still come around are pretty special. But this place. These old frame walls. Nothing special about them, Will. They're just wood and plaster and probably some termites!"

Will surrendered. Right or wrong, Maggie Day had made up her mind.

"Okay, Miss . . . I mean, Maggie. So what can I do for you this morning? Whatever you say, I'm your man. My treat."

Maggie smiled. "Let's have ourselves a good old time, Will. Unless Lanny wanders in here, I suspect we'll have the place to ourselves. So let's find some music on the radio, take down the rest of the pictures, pack away the dishes, and . . ." she paused, thinking, "we're done!"

"We might get some stragglers."

Maggie laughed. "If we do, we'll make 'em wash dishes and cook for themselves! But don't hold your breath, Will Joseph. Don't hold your breath."

Mention of Lanny Hargrave had started Will wondering about their unofficial charge. He was Holly Day's last regular.

"You think Lanny's okay out there by himself?"

"I think Lanny's a growed man. He knows to get in out of the weather."

"What did Lanny ever do to make Frank treat him so bad?"

Maggie ceased her counter work. She looked at Will and smiled. "Lanny was just Lanny. That wasn't enough for Frank . . . not after his mom died."

"Well, I mean, Lanny's not much of a talker—I gotta admit—and he doesn't dress so well, but he's a decent enough guy."

"That's 'cause you're a real decent kid *and* 'cause Lanny's not your daddy."

Will dropped the topic and started taking stock of the food on hand. He counted milk and eggs and packages of bacon and loaves of bread.

"We don't have much food in."

"You don't think it'll get us through lunch?"

"I don't mean for us! I mean if anybody stops over 'cause of the snow."

"Will," Maggie slapped her towel over the counter, "how many times do I have to tell you . . . nobody . . . I repeat, nobody's . . . going to come here just 'cause of a big snow. Besides, what's it look like we're doing? We're closed!"

"I don't know," Will stared out the window at the unceasing snow, "you just wait and see, Maggie. You just wait and see!"

"Will, nobody's comin' in *my* place if I don't want 'em to!"

CHAPTER 4

Because They Need Us

ZECHARIAH YOUNG FOLDED HIS TROUSERS, smoothing every wrinkle, straightening every line. Then he placed them carefully inside his leather valise. Elizabeth watched from the edge of the bed. His motions were slow, methodical, determined, as if performed for an audience of entranced observers. After the trousers came his shirts, then his underwear, his socks, a belt, his shave kit, and finally a faded wool sweater. The weatherman on WCHR was just concluding. It had been the first station Liz found on the small clock radio next to their bed. She simply wanted Zech to listen and follow his common sense for a change.

"We spent one night in this motel, we can spend two, Zech." Her voice was suggestive but not pleading, firm but not carping. She had lived with Zech Young for over fifty years and she could tell when she might as well be speaking to a wall. He didn't answer, continuing instead to tidy up in preparation for check-out.

When he had finished with all of his clean clothes he turned to her. "You would have us stay in a motel room on Christmas Eve?"

Liz threw her hands in the air. "Zech Young, you hypocrite! I can not believe what I am hearing. Tell me you have not made Christmas an excuse for driving into a blizzard!"

He returned to his suitcase, separating the dirty socks from the clean, the shirt he wore the day before from the one encased in the dry cleaner's plastic bag. Motion. Any motion that would distract him from her familiar barbs. Then he turned. "I've always liked Christmas. Irving Berlin wrote 'White Christmas.'"

"You wouldn't drive in a blizzard for Hanukkah!"

"Bing Crosby didn't sing 'I'm dreaming of a white Hanukkah.' If he had, it might be different. Besides, your daughter-in-law is Presbyterian and so is your granddaughter—and she wants to see her grandparents on Christmas Eve."

"That's not it and you know it! Besides, nobody's been pushing for us to visit during the holidays."

"But she hasn't *not* been pushing and that's very important."

"You are nuts, old man, nuts!" Liz was no longer the stoic mate of an inveterate eccentric.

"Now we're calling names, are we? Well, you stay if you want to, but I'm not afraid of a little bad weather. Not when it comes to family!"

He stared at her, waiting for a response. She pressed her tongue defiantly between her teeth and lips and remained silent. Then she stood up and flipped on the television. Willard Scott stood in a Santa Claus outfit, predicting bad weather throughout the entire Southeast.

"So say something." He blocked the TV screen.

"What is there to say? You've made up your mind."

"Say what you're thinking."

"It won't do me any good."

"You never know if you don't try."

"You don't want to hear what I have to say."

"If I didn't want to hear it, I wouldn't have asked you to say it! Now please, stop being difficult."

Another moment of silence while she contemplated her words. She took a breath, then held it for a second. She wanted to make him listen. She didn't want to hurt him. She wondered what she could say that would do good instead of harm. For fifty years of marriage she had been peevish with Zech Young and he with her. Their constant, often comical, carping had become an expected attraction at a party or over dinner or even at temple when they attended. But this was beyond peevishness. For weeks, maybe even months, he had become increasingly agitated. The dream condo in Sarasota had become a prison. The beautiful weather had become bland and uninteresting. Retirement had been transformed from rest and relaxation into a life sentence. Nothing pleased him. Nothing except the memories of what the business had once been like in Louisville, Owensboro, and Bowling Green.

When the old tales were trotted out over dinner or when one of their remaining friends dropped by to chat, Zech invariably turned the conversation to retailing as he had known it.

"Okay, Zech Young. I will be honest. Honest so it hurts. Your children love you, your grandchildren love you, but they don't care if you arrive today, tomorrow, or next week. Stanley is dreading your arrival."

"Has he told you that?"

"Of course not, but what do you expect? It's his tenth year in the business. The economy is awful. He's laying people off, changing the image of the stores . . ."

"There's one mistake for sure!"

". . . and he's got a know-it-all father who wants to run the business like he did thirty years ago."

"Thirty years ago it worked well enough to make money for his college and business school . . . a lot of good that did!"

"Let up on him. Let him work things out with his sister. When they were little you never let them work things out, and now look at them."

"That's right. They need me again. You've answered my question. We're leaving today. We're two hours away from them. Just two hours."

"It could be two days in that stuff!"

"We could get ahead of it."

"Look outside! It's already ahead of *us!*"

"They need me, Liz. They need us."

She wanted to ignore the pleading in his voice, but couldn't. "Zech, they haven't said they need us at all."

"That's right. They haven't *said* they need us. They haven't said a thing. And if you were listening you would know that silence speaks louder than any words!"

"I have been listening. And sometimes I think you talk in riddles. If they wanted us they wouldn't remain silent. They're intelligent adults. They can speak for themselves."

"Not when they're acting like children, and, Liz, they have been acting like very young, very ill-behaved children."

"Maybe you're right. Maybe they need you to come in and make peace. But Zech, it will wait twenty-four hours. One day out of the year. That's all."

"And how many days do I have left? Eh?"

"Don't start in on that again." Liz wagged her finger at Zech, but her heart had leaped to a familiar place in the back of her throat.

"The doctor said you never know how long these things may take. I may have a few months . . ."

"You may have another twenty years. Now stop it. I don't want to hear about your prostate again."

"You don't want to hear! God robs me of my manhood and you would still my cries!"

"You're full of baloney! Your manhood is intact . . ."

"Well, maybe so, but I don't appreciate your making light like that."

"So you really think you can bring them peace—*shalom*?"

"I don't know. I can try."

Liz shook her head. For all of his hardheadedness Zech had always been the more indulgent, the more idealistic, the more romantic of the two.

"You've got a lot of faith in yourself, Zechariah Young."

He paused before closing his suitcase. Then he let down the lid and faced her.

"Truth be told, I have very little faith. Least of all in myself. If I had more faith I wouldn't have dragged us out of Sarasota in the middle of the winter! I feel like some migrating bird who's lost." Zech's voice weakened. "If I had just a little faith I might not feel like I did the wrong thing years ago."

"You did the right thing."

"I raised two children who eat each other alive."

"You can't control events."

"I can try."

Liz came to him, placing her hand on his knee. "So now it's God I'm married to? Or Moses on the mount?"

"Moses didn't control things either . . . but he tried. He tried because he loved his children. I love mine."

"Ours." She sighed and patted his knee. "I love them enough to let them settle their own crises."

"Then you stay here. I'll go on alone. I'll rent a car. Or I can come back and get you."

"You don't mean that." Her voice was soft, understanding.

"I do. I do mean it."

"No, you don't."

Zech shook his head. She wasn't the least bit shaken by him. She could see right through him. Her immunity to his threats spanned decades. He lowered his outstretched arms to his side.

"No," he said. "I don't mean that. I wouldn't go without you. I couldn't and I wouldn't." Zech looked down at his gnarled hands as if they held some secret in their creases. "But I need to go home. I need to be there for them."

Liz sighed. She had lost the argument and she knew it. She could never stay behind when he was on a mission, and for him, saving the business was a mission. She could never tell Zech to simply go on without her.

"Sometimes you can be foolish old man . . . but never a fool. I have not loved a fool for fifty years."

"That's comforting," he smiled.

"If you're going, then I'll go with you. My bags are already packed."

His eyes thickened with tears. He stuck out his thick lower lip and stared at the ceiling, then away to the snow falling steadily outside the window of their ground-floor room. She watched him slowly put on his overcoat, turn out the light by their bed, and pick up their bags.

❄ ❄ ❄ ❄ ❄ ❄ ❄ ❄ ❄

"This old baby'll churn this snow up like cornmeal," Jake Masters grinned.

Becky smiled and nodded, nestling down in the passenger seat of their faded gray Impala. The air flowing from under the dash was a mixture of odors—creaking vinyl and musty upholstery, the dust of softball fields and the reminders of perfumed Saturday nights, the freshness of hay and the hint of fall leaves. They were the smells of home and they made her happy.

She glanced into the back seat. Little Jake was asleep, his baby's chin drooling, his neck crooked at an odd angle. He was smiling, dreaming. They were all happy, Becky thought. "On the road to opportunity." That's what Jake had said. It had a ring to it like poetry and she believed him. She believed almost everything he said. He was older than her—almost twenty-two—and she'd always respected that.

Becky closed her eyes and remembered their first kiss. The brush of Jake's cheek, the scent of his Aqua Velva, his wet, full lips playing against hers, his arm over her shoulder as he squeezed her to him, the movie's sound track filling the car. She was propped right against the Impala's passenger door, halfway through the second feature at the Skyview Drive-In. No one was watching. She wouldn't have cared if they were. She was in love with Jake Masters and proud of it.

It was in the back seat where he asked her to marry him just before the start of her senior year. She had said yes. Jake was working for Bluebird Trucking and the future stretched on forever. She left school to start making a home, just as her mother had. A year later Little Jake came along, just when Bluebird was going out of business.

"Hungry?" Jake's question jolted her. The snow had hypnotized her, freeing her mind to wander over times past.

"Hungry?" she repeated. "Not unless you are. I can wait."

"We won't get there 'til way after noon in this stuff."

"I'm not hungry." She was, but she wasn't going to admit it. "Little Jake's lunch is right here in the bag."

"Stuff's slick," Jake continued. She wondered if he was scared. She'd never seen Jake scared of anything. She wanted to show him she wasn't either, even if she was.

"You can handle it," she smiled. He smiled in return. Jake melted whenever she reminded him of his skills as a driver, an athlete, a husband, and a father.

"I don't know," he said. There was a catch in his voice. He was concerned. The chassis of the Chevy caught a gust of wind and wavered from side to side.

"Maybe we should've put those chains on before we left."

He laughed, but his voice cracked. "Chains aren't for highways, darling." Then he paused, pinching his nose. "'Cept this ain't no highway anymore, so maybe you're right!"

Neither Jake nor Becky spoke after that. Becky tried to relax but couldn't. "This ain't no highway anymore." His words recurred to her. Then what was it? A long white road into hell, she thought. Christmas was no time to be traveling on roads like this. Christmas was no time to be traveling, period. Her parents had begged them to stay on the farm. Good warm bed, good warm food, a fireplace. Love. Everything they needed—except a job for Jake. That's why Jake had to drive north, and he had to be there that afternoon to show the company he was serious. And there was no way she and the baby were going to let him travel alone on Christmas Eve. Besides, maybe some tough old boss might see her and the baby waiting in the car. Then Jake would get the job. He better.

❄ ❄ ❄ ❄ ❄ ❄ ❄ ❄ ❄

Marie Thomas realized the insanity of inching northward into a blizzard. She should have headed south. Gone to the beach with friends. They wouldn't have cared back home. They were busy with things. Work. Ski clubs. Hobbies. Theater. Causes. They filled their lives with things and barely worried about her. They said they cared. They even came to the first parents' weekend. But that just proved they liked Nashville. She was crazy to be going home. Crazier still in the snow.

She fumbled in her purse for a cigarette and failed. The car drifted and she put both hands on the wheel. She was having a hard time picking up another bad habit. Nearly wrecked twice groping for the lighter. Give up, she thought. It didn't do much for her anyway.

So if not a cigarette, then what? The ever-slowing, slug-like lines of traffic were driving her nuts. She gripped the leather-wrapped wheel of her Porsche even harder and let out a groan. The little space inside the car was toasty and she needed sleep. The expressway was neither the time nor the place. She forced her eyes to stay open. In the same instant she wondered what it would be like if she let it happen. She would drift off, enjoy the peace of dreams, then the inevitable crash. What if she didn't die? She might end up a paraplegic. No, she'd pick her time if it came to that.

Marie cracked the window. Cold air and snowflakes blew over her. That was better. Better to be awake. She wouldn't hurt anyone else that way either. That was important.

She didn't even know if she'd go back second semester. No matter what she decided to do, the time off might be good. She could hang out in Chicago until summer. Then she'd see where things were. And if things weren't where they should be, well, she'd regroup.

She reached over and changed the fading channel on the radio. WCHR was all that crackled through the static. More snow . . . all day . . . unpredictable into the night . . . a record-breaker for Kentucky.

"Just a red-letter day all around," she muttered. It was a phrase her grandfather often used. She wasn't sure what it meant. "Kentucky," she laughed. "What a hick state!"

The Porsche shimmied. Mind back on the road. Maybe Kentucky had taken offence. It would serve her right. She was one to be calling names! She'd taken a steady diet of self-deprecation for two weeks: stupid, careless, foolish, dumb. The words all ran together. She couldn't stop them. She wasn't even sure she wanted to. Her closest friends—they were the ones who knew—said it wouldn't be so bad. Just make a decision and go from there. The conversations replayed in her head but she couldn't buy it. It wasn't that easy.

What would her father say? She couldn't tell him. She was his girl—the oldest, the dependable, the reliable, the one who had kept a handle on things: clothes and car and trips abroad had been tempered with common sense and school honors and good grades. She was the one he counted on to make something of herself. And her mother? She would have to tell her—eventually. And she would have to listen to the tears and the disclaimers of her own failures as a mother. But then her mother would settle down, stop worrying about the impression it would make on the members at the club, and consider solutions. Bad as it might be, her mother's reaction would be easier to handle than her father's.

There was a rest stop just ahead. She'd made it up the big hill out of Tennessee and into Kentucky. Maybe the worst was over. Maybe the snow would quit, maybe the road crews would be at work, maybe she'd find a McDonald's and get a cup of coffee.

CHAPTER 5

Pilgrims Adrift

By TEN, MAGGIE WAS SURE she would be snowbound and alone by Christmas Eve night. She had practically ordered Will gone by noon. Then the front door blew open and started the old spring bell ringing. Maggie jumped and Will dropped the ashtray he was wiping out.

"Well Maggie, looks like you're the only act in town!"

The state trooper stomped his boots on the welcome mat and dusted the snow off his khaki parka. He was red-faced and grinning, ice dripping from his thick mustache.

"I'm closed and why don't you just scare us half to death barging in here like John Wayne!" Maggie's words came rat-tat-tat. The tall man looked around as if to see who was the object of her mock wrath. "Well, if you're staying, close the door!" she added.

"Merry Christmas to you too . . . rest a while . . . taste my coffee . . . glad to see you . . . and how-do-you-do! But what do you mean, closed?"

"I mean closed—decided last night."

"Nah, Maggie . . ."

"Now, stop your whining, Buddy."

"Queen of the put down, Maggie . . . long live the Queen!"

"And don't forget it, Buddy boy!" Then she broke into an eye-winking grin. "I just don't want Mr. Radio to have it go to his head."

"You heard me?" He was undaunted by her acid tongue. He had grown up on it.

"You bet I did. You're big time now!"

"Did I sound okay?" He didn't let Maggie answer. "What did you think, Will?"

"Sorry, Buddy, I missed it."

"You were the best state trooper on WCHR so far today!" Maggie added.

"Well, thanks, Maggie . . ." he began, then got the jibe. "Oh . . . I get it . . . and the only trooper on WCHR . . . right. Very funny."

"Come on. Come on." Maggie sashayed from behind the counter and put her arm around Buddy. "You were my boy ten years ago—just like Mr. Joseph over there—and you're still my boy." Buddy grinned. "That's better," she continued. "One thing Maggie Day always teaches her boys is how to take a joke." Maggie kissed him on the cheek. "It's awful good of you to drop by and see an old woman on her last days . . . here in Christian." She hadn't meant for it to come out that way. Buddy and Will stared at her. She let it pass. "Now, what's happening out there?"

"It's bad, Maggie. Real bad. If it gets any worse we're closing down the expressways."

"Hallelujah!" Maggie crowed. "I've been trying to close 'em for the last six governors. Never figured I paid them enough . . . but nature came through for me."

"I'm serious, Maggie." Buddy ignored her sarcasm. His mind and words were a jumble of things done and yet to be done.

"Okay, I'll be serious too—but only for a few seconds. So what are 'ya doing here if it's so bad out there?"

"Well, I don't know, Maggie, I thought I'd get a cup of coffee at least, even if you are closed."

"Did 'ya hear that, Will? A pay customer . . . and he's too late. 'Course with Buddy as a customer it might just be enough to get you started in business!"

"Will's buying the place?" Buddy broke in. "That's great . . ."

"Over my dead body. It's a joke, Buddy."

"I never did get your jokes, Maggie."

"But I loved you anyway, Buddy." Maggie shuffled back around the counter. "Now, here's your coffee."

"Maybe I better get a go cup."

Buddy slapped a fifty-cent piece on the counter. Maggie flipped it back at him and he caught it.

"No charge today, Buddy. Drinks on the house." She wondered if he would still love her if the place suddenly burned down. Just a little spontaneous combustion. She tried not to think of it.

"I'll take it, Maggie, but only `cause you're a friend. But don't be surprised if you get some customers today."

"Not today. You and Lanny were my last customers yesterday."

"Did ya see Lanny out there?" Will interrupted.

"Been too busy working to look out for Lanny. But I know where he is."

"At Lanny's Overlook," Will added.

"You got it. Even in a blizzard. The man don't quit."

"Sometimes you gotta quit." Maggie's voice fell but Buddy didn't notice. He was still focused on Lanny.

"Lanny'll quit waitin' and watchin' the day Frank walks through that door." Buddy sipped his coffee.

"Which'll be never," Will added knowingly.

"You never know." Maggie had no conviction in her voice. She didn't believe Frank Hargrave would ever return to Christian, but she liked to argue.

Buddy laughed, then looked around at the empty booths and chipped formica tables, the ancient juke box, the dusty upright, and the silent wood stove. "I'm sorry you're leaving, Maggie. We'll miss you."

"There'll be someone else here."

"It won't be the same."

"I appreciate the thought, Buddy, but we haven't exactly been breakin' attendance records 'round here lately."

Buddy ignored her. "We'll miss you, Maggie." Buddy finished his coffee with a gulp and put the go cup down for a refill. "One more to remember you by. I gotta get back on the road."

"Be careful, Buddy." Maggie's voice lowered as she dropped her guard. "Snow's as slick for you as it is for them."

❋ ❋ ❋ ❋ ❋ ❋ ❋ ❋ ❋ ❋

One look out the window of the rest stop and Leo DeAngelis knew the expressway would be closed by noon. He knew it without the news from WCHR. Leo tugged his beard, straining away the melting ice. He flicked his hand downward, then rearranged his Mack Truck cap. The steam from his coffee wafted up and he took comfort. The deep, rich smell made him think of home. Home was wherever he pulled the rig over for the night. Sometimes home was full of fun, sometimes somber, sometimes welcome, sometimes not. But the coffee was always hot and it was nearly always good. Coffee was always a comfort.

Leo fidgeted towards decision, already knowing that he would leave. The crowd packed in around him wasn't so sure. They stood in lines for the pay phones, milled through the bathrooms, and huddled around the drinking fountains and candy machines, trading rumors about the weather. Not Leo. He had a deadline and an unsympathetic shipper. Less than a hundred yards away his rig stood running in the cold, belching diesel exhaust at the gray swollen clouds, beckoning like a mount ready for battle. Even if he should let it chug away for another hour or two, he wouldn't. He was ready to leave.

If it weren't for the deadline he would just as soon stay. The rest stop was warm, the hot water and toilets worked, and there was plenty of food in the rig. The storm would pass. It was a freak. And if it didn't, well then he could wait. Christmas was just another day.

"Roads look pretty bad out there." The old man at his side nodded as if he had said something important.

"Worst in years," Leo mumbled.

"Zech, ask the man what he knows about the road ahead." The woman seemed hesitant to talk to the bearded trucker.

Zech looked back at Liz in irritation, then turned to Leo. "What do you hear about the roads?"

"Not good anywhere north of here . . . far as I know." Leo resumed his watch on the road, moving a pinch of snuff from one cheek to the other.

"See, Zech." The woman waved her finger once for emphasis.

"Mister," the old man's voice had softened to a plea, "we've got to get up the road. What are you going to do?"

Leo turned to him. "Well, I'll tell you. I've got a whole trailer full of Florida oranges. Due tonight. If I wait up and they freeze, they won't be good for anything but juice. Then I'm out a load."

"You're going?" the old man persisted.

"I'm going." Leo nodded toward the northern sky. "Don't know how far, but I can't wait here."

"You see!" The old man's voice quavered.

"I wouldn't go if I were you." Leo lowered his voice so the old woman wouldn't hear.

"I've gotta go." The old man matched the teamster's hush.

"Your choice," Leo noted without inflection. The last thing he needed was an old man and woman using him as their excuse for starting out.

"I heard you all talking. Are you leaving soon?" Marie Thomas nudged toward the three. Snow had driven her to the rest stop as well.

"Soon as I finish this cup of coffee," Leo shook his head, "but don't you all follow me. I can move through this stuff a little different than a car." He eyed the girl all bundled up in an expensive fur. Little rich college girl going home. Some people got it made, he thought.

"But if we follow you, there'll be a path." She pulled the fur tighter around her. "I need to get home . . . I really need to get home."

Leo slid the brim of his cap between his thumb and forefinger. The three of them were making him nervous. "Folks, I'm leaving. What you do is your business."

He pitched the remainder of his coffee and pulled his old plaid fleece around him. The lamb's wool brushed softly against his hair. The sooner he could get out the door the less likely they'd follow. His big rubber-soled boots thumped as his body heaved forward. In a second he was out the door.

"Liz, we're going." Zech grabbed his wife's hand and before she knew it they were out in the snow again.

Marie Thomas began to panic. No one had invited her along. She could follow or she could stay. No matter to them. She fumbled for a cigarette, secured and lit it. She inhaled, her mind racing, her fingers twitching, the muscles in the back of her neck tensing. The longer things went unsettled, the worse it was for everyone. She searched the crowd, half hoping for one of the indecisives to take command. They continued to mill around, looking at their watches, fretting over the sky. If she didn't follow the truck driver and the old couple, there was no telling when she'd get away. She took one last drag of her cigarette, coughed, and put it out. She shoved the bar of the front door and ran outside to catch up with them.

❄ ❄ ❄ ❄ ❄ ❄ ❄ ❄ ❄ ❄

The small of Sarah's back tightened. Her head had been pounding for the last hour. The last gust of wind had sent their Toyota gliding left then right. The snow was sticking like cold oatmeal on the wipers. A bad situation was becoming a disaster. When the wheels of the car stopped shimmying she exhaled and tried to recompose before the cycle repeated itself. Forty miles and over two hours ago they had left Nashville. Every inch had been a battle, but she still plodded up the road.

"How much longer, Mommy?" Julie asked. She had asked ten times already. Five times in the last fifteen minutes. Sarah had counted.

"A lot longer, Julie. I told you we shouldn't leave in the storm." Sarah bit her lower lip. Now she was blaming Julie for decisions that were hers and hers alone. She could have said no to Julie. The world wouldn't have ended. It would end now if she made a mistake.

Julie fiddled with the radio. The FM band was a blanket of static, differing only in degrees. The constant sizzle began to grate on Sarah.

"Don't play with that, pumpkin."

"Why?"

"Because I said so, that's why!" Sarah's voice jumped up an octave as she felt the car lurch. Her eyes locked on the road ahead. Julie grew silent. She finally understood the problem, the relationship of the snow to the road, and the road to the car.

Sarah wanted to be home and warm. And she wanted the company of a man who understood her—or, at least, tried.

Her last date of two weeks before had been anything but understanding when she spoke of her hassles with Julie's father. "You sound like the poster girl for N.O.W."

"You mean poster woman." She had tried to keep it light.

"Very funny."

"I thought so. A touch of self-deprecation is always a clever touch."

He had shifted the conversation to movies, books, and sports. The evening had ended with a perfunctory kiss. She'd never see him again. Just as well.

Sarah hadn't seen another car for miles. Just snow. Blinding, debilitating snow. Now there were suddenly cars. Not one, nor two, but three. All following a tractor-trailer. She found herself behind a beaten-up old Chevy. Exhaust belched from its rear. The world was gray and washed out. The car was gray and washed out. In front of the Chevy there was some type of sports car. It was mostly hidden by the Chevy's skirts. In front of the sports car was another big car, newer than the Chevy. It looked like a Cadillac. She couldn't tell. But they were all going slow, spewing snow, grinding away the miles behind the semi.

Sarah followed the trail left by their tires. She didn't have any choice. Passing was suicide. The slush from the Chevy's rear wheels slung up on her hood and windshield. Her wipers weren't keeping up. Her back tightened even more and her head throbbed.

Christmas plans had been a mistake from the beginning. She

knew that now. She should have left two nights before, giving herself time to break from work and prepare for the holidays. The university had been out since the end of exams. Most of the staff had sneaked out after noon on Friday. They weren't coming back until after New Year's. Why hadn't she taken the extra time off? Sarah laughed to herself. She had never taken the easy way, why start in the face of natural disaster? And why so stubborn? Pride. She knew the answer before the question formed. She could and would show *him.* He had asked for Julie earlier during the holidays. He had been flexible. He had always been flexible and it had always served his purpose. It made her look bad. Not this time, she thought. This time she was making the extra effort. So here she was, shoulders yoked in her seat belt, static the only music crackling out of the car speakers.

An overpass loomed ahead. She saw a pickup truck stopped. A white-haired man was standing on the overpass, shouting something. She strained to hear. She slowed and rolled down her window.

"Get off!" His shouting was more like a whisper in the wind.

"What's he saying?" Julie asked.

"He's saying 'get off.'" Sarah tried to think and talk and stay calm at the same time. What did he mean? Who was he? Was the old man crazy? She wondered if something had happened ahead. The road began to feel even slicker than before. In one instant her stubbornness told her to plod on. In the next instant she remembered her thoughts of a second before.

She couldn't see the exit sign, but she could tell that the road was branching off. She veered to the right, trying to pick her way from markers and snow-covered signs. At ten miles an hour it felt like they were traveling in a dream, but she could tell there was road beneath her. For once in her life simple fear had won out over stubbornness. She was glad to surrender.

❄ ❄ ❄ ❄ ❄ ❄ ❄ ❄ ❄ ❄

Lanny Hargrave parked his old Dodge pickup on the overpass, its six cylinders purring in the cold. Hot air belched out of the vents above the floorboards. It was cold outside, toasty in the old cab. He sat perched in his usual spot where he could see the cars and trucks rolling north and south on the expressway. It was his spot, his crow's nest for watching for Frank. Lanny didn't mind that the locals called it Lanny's Overpass—even Maggie and Will did. From his overpass Lanny could see everything that traveled below. If Frank's car came along, he'd know it. It would be a tan and green company car with the John Deere logo on the side.

The old engine stuttered, then perked back up. With the needle nearly on empty he couldn't stay much longer. Another ten minutes and he would move on to Holly Day's. No use staying longer. Traffic was thinning out, even on the expressway. More so as the clouds dumped more snow. Lanny smiled. There was an advantage to fewer cars and trucks. Not as many to stare at. Green and tan— always looking for green and tan. Before too long they'd be crawling north and south. If Frank was on the road he'd have to get off with the rest. Lanny was patient. Through the weeks and months and years he had been infinitely patient. Sooner or later Frank would pass beneath. Then Lanny would catch him. Coming or going. Sooner or later.

The trouble was that all the vehicles were beginning to look alike. They were beginning to look like a convoy of snow tanks, covered in white with little wipers maintaining peepholes in the front. The Mercedes began to look like Oldsmobiles and the BMWs like Toyotas. Lanny smiled again. Nature was the great leveler. Maybe his '62 Dodge was beginning to look like a new Ram. Not likely.

The smile from his last thought faded as he saw trouble below. A semi, a big old Lincoln or Caddy, some sort of sports car, and a broad old Chevy or Buick approached from the south. The semi had started to slow down, then shimmy. The roads had turned from slush to ice since Lanny had been sitting on the overpass. But if the semi realized what lay ahead, the sports car didn't. It was passing in the left lane. First it passed the Caddy, then drew alongside the semi. The semi tried to pull over even farther to the right to give it room, then its rear swung out and the cab pinched in. They went under the overpass. Lanny jumped out of his pickup and waded through the snow to the opposite rail. When he got there the semi was sliding sideways like some child's toy down the length of both north-bound lanes. The sports car was spinning like a top. Lanny couldn't watch. He rushed back across the overpass to see what had happened to the others. The Caddy and the old Chevy were just going under, slowing down, but spinning as well.

"Get off," he yelled uselessly into the wind. "Get off." The exit was just past the overpass. Lanny saw another car approaching. Some sort of compact. It was slowing down.

"Get off," he screamed, arms flailing. "Get off!"

This time the car slowed as if it had noticed him. A window rolled down.

"Get off!" Lanny bellowed one more time as the compact went

under him. He ran back across the road and watched it glide gradually off the expressway to the right. He had saved it. He had saved it. "Damn!" Lanny yelled in exultation. "They listened, they did. They listened!"

❋ ❋ ❋ ❋ ❋ ❋ ❋ ❋ ❋ ❋

When Leo felt the road give out from beneath him, it was too late to pull the rig back around. The only thing he could do was let the road take him along and try to keep turning his wheels into the slide. In the same instant the slide began he saw the Porsche trying to pass on the left. If it lost control, it would go under the trailer. If it did, the driver was dead. He had a heartbeat to act. He threw the gears on the tractor and as it began to slowly twist around the Porsche, Leo felt his body sway, first to his left then his right—no contact, no collision. But when Leo tried to bring the tractor back under control it was like spinning the wheel on a child's toy. The trailer started careening down the highway like an errant hockey puck, the cab headed straight for an abutment.

CHAPTER 6

The First Pilgrims Arrive

THE DOOR OPENED AGAIN, its clanging bell muted by the screams of Lanny Hargrave. He ran straight for Buddy Wendell.

"Quick, Buddy . . . there's a wreck. It's bad. Real bad . . ." Lanny's chest heaved in and out.

"Slow down, Lanny. What are you talking about? What wreck? Where?"

"On the northbound . . . just past the overpass. Big rig's twisted round with a bunch of cars."

Buddy looked at Maggie for a sign. She could always tell if Lanny had been drinking. She took one look and knew he was sober. "Better go, Buddy. Sounds like real trouble." Buddy zipped up his officer-blue down coat then grabbed up his gloves.

"I'll go with you." Will started for his old plaid coat.

"You stay here with Maggie. Goes for you too, Lanny. I'll call the post if I need help." The trooper yanked his hat on tight and headed for the door.

"Be careful, Buddy. You hear?" Maggie called after him, but he was already gone.

"Buddy's a good man." Will nodded in the direction of the state trooper's four-by-four careening away from the café.

"The best," Maggie exhaled. "Don't you ever tell him I told you," she added softly.

"Why don't *you* tell him?"

Maggie didn't answer. She walked to the door and stared out at the storm. The snow had swallowed him up in a haze of zigzagging crystals. She set her jaw. It was time for action. She couldn't follow Buddy. There wasn't anyone else to call for help. Lanny would settle down and be okay, but she had to do something. There were people in trouble and they might need her. Need her. The thought of being needed felt strange, yet at the same time it was familiar, like the face of an acquaintance from years before whose name has long since been forgotten. She strained to recollect what was required.

"Will, go to the register. Take out fifty dollars . . . no, seventy-five. Go to John's for groceries. If he's closed, get him to open up."

"Groceries?"

"You remember what those are! Get some ground beef and buns, a couple of steaks, and a couple of chicken breasts. Grab a pound of rice and some baked beans and some tomato sauce and spaghetti. Pick up some fresh fruit if he's got it. Get some milk and bread and eggs. Spend the rest on whatever you think we'll need."

"What rest are you talking about? There won't be anything left!" Will paused, thinking. "You think we're gonna get a crowd?"

"Maybe. Don't know. But if Buddy needs us to help somehow, we're going to do it. Now go on, Will, before we have to eat each other!"

Will hopped over the counter and took the money from the register. An instant later he was at the door. He jerked it open and a woman and a little girl all but fell into the café. They looked dazed by the cold and the snow.

"Here's the first pilgrims!" Maggie called out.

Julie returned Maggie's country girl grin, but Sarah's stare was colder than the weather. Maggie moved over to extend a hand. Sarah nodded and clutched her arms about her in a shiver. Maggie knew she was in for trouble.

"Don't like pilgrims?"

Maggie's attempt at a joke flopped. Sarah's brows closed.

"I beg your pardon?" Sarah's voice cut like a scalpel once her teeth stopped chattering.

"I said, here's the first pilgrims . . . hope you ain't prejudiced against pilgrims!" Maggie's expression was deadpan. She suddenly remembered that most pay customers didn't have a sense of humor. Not like hers, anyway.

"No problem." Sarah stared all around. Maggie followed her eyes and read her thoughts: "Ptomaine tavern . . . bug-infested joint . . . more grease than the pits at Indy." There would be no pleasing this one.

The little girl was at least direct. "Can I get a Big Mac?"

Maggie laughed. The little girl was okay. Maybe she'd keep her and pitch the other one out.

"No hon, you might find a Tough Buddy or an Old Lanny and this here's Skinny Will, but no Big Macs!"

"Is this a restaurant, or an inn, or what?" Sarah's voice was beyond condescension.

"It's a café—Holly Day's Café . . . Will's just about to make a food run . . . you're welcome to wait or you can leave. 'Course there's no place between here and the nearest town, and the nearest town's about fifty miles north of here."

"We can't wait. We've got to be in Cincinnati tonight—at the latest."

"No problem," Maggie added almost gleefully. "Suit yourself."

Will had started for groceries several times but hesitated, ready to intercede if Maggie's patience ran thin. The woman and her little girl were real customers and the café could use a little business to liven things up.

"Ma'am, I don't think you have much choice. There's been a wreck on the expressway . . ."

"Wreck?" Sarah turned to her daughter. "That's what he was trying to tell us."

"'He' who?" Maggie interjected.

"Some crazy-looking guy," Sarah began. "He had a wild beard and longish hair . . . an old hat and coat . . ."

Lanny was sitting in a booth behind them, catching his breath and regrouping from the excitement. He shifted uncomfortably and took another sip of the coffee he had served himself seconds before. His movement caught Julie's eye and she tried to get her mother's attention before she went on any longer.

". . . he was motioning for us to get off and he looked half drunk," Sarah continued and so did Julie. Her persistent tugging finally paid off. Sarah looked down at her daughter then toward the man in the booth. Her thoughts and words trailed off, then after a second of silence she looked up at Maggie. "That's the man."

"Crazy old Lanny Hargrave!" Maggie observed sarcastically. "One of the worst dressed men in Christian . . ." Maggie paused, enjoying Sarah's embarrassment. "Lanny, I'd like you to meet two of our fine patrons today . . . Let's see, there's . . ."

". . . Julie Herald," Sarah added quickly, "and I'm her mother, Sarah."

"Glad to meet you," Lanny added.

"Yessir, Lanny, you're liable to have saved these folks lives today . . . but you're right, Mrs. Herald, he's no Cary Grant."

"Please, just call me Sarah."

"Long as we're being sociable then, my name's Maggie, Maggie Day. This is my associate, Mr. Will Joseph. This is a restaurant. We are serving food and Will was just leaving." She motioned Will to leave. "Now, if you want to stay a while, you're welcome."

"Well, I need to use the phone no matter what."

"It's over there."

Sarah went straight for the phone, leaving Julie with Maggie. Lanny continued to stare out the window from his booth. Sensing that a frail truce had formed between Maggie and Sarah, Will nodded good-bye and left.

"Where are y'all heading on such an awful day, Julie?" Maggie liked Julie. She winked at the little girl and leaned toward her across the counter.

"To see my daddy in Cincinnati," Julie answered in her best grown-up voice.

"For Christmas?"

"Yep."

"Why doesn't he just come to see you?"

"He said he would, but Mommy says that's not their agreement."

"A deal's a deal! Right? Am I right?" Maggie raised her brows.

"That's exactly what she said!" Julie's eyes widened at Maggie's knowledge.

"I'll bet your Mom's not too happy about these roads right now." Maggie nodded down the hall where Sarah stood at the phone, hands flailing up and down, her jaw jutting out as she spoke.

"She's not happy about anything lately. Not since Daddy asked the judge for joint custody."

"You're a pretty smart little girl."

"You've got to stay on top of things these days."

Maggie threw her head back and laughed. Then she slapped her towel down on the counter. This kid was okay. She was bright and sharp. Almost too sharp. But she was going to grow up to be okay.

As Maggie patted Julie on the shoulder, Sarah slammed down the receiver and stamped her foot in anger. Maggie resolved not to say a word as Sarah returned from her call. Julie did instead.

"What did Daddy say?"

Sarah looked away. She had no intention of hearing herself emote in front of Maggie and Lanny whatever his name was.

Maggie read her thoughts and turned around, fiddling with the dials on the radio and wiping the chrome counter at the pass-through window.

"I'll tell you later."

"Tell me now!"

"I said later!"

"Tell me now. Please tell me."

"He wants to come down here and I told him no!"

"But if Daddy comes here . . ."

"I don't need Magic Man skimming in on snow skis!" Sarah's voice turned shrill. Her jaw locked shut.

"Your mom's right about that, Julie. Nobody's getting in or getting out of Christian for the rest of the day at least."

"Thank you!" Sarah half-huffed at Maggie. Maggie read her insincerity. What she clearly meant was, "Thank you, but I don't need your help."

Maggie's eyes locked with Sarah's. Neither woman blinked. Sarah was nowhere close to Maggie's idea of a model customer. Better the café be dark and silent than filled with the collective anger of Sarah's bad marriage. If Sarah wanted to scream at her former husband on the phone, fine, but Maggie would be damned if she'd let Sarah take it out on her.

"Sarah, can I have a word with you for a second?"

"Anything we say can be said . . ."

"No," Maggie's no was soft but nonnegotiable. "This is my place—humble though it may be—and I would like to see you over here in my conference corner for just a second." Maggie's sarcasm wasn't lost on Sarah. Sarah might not agree with Maggie, but she recognized that she was on Maggie's turf. She wet her lips, closed her eyes slightly, and said, "Of course." Then she asked Julie to go look at the old juke box while she spoke to Ms. Day alone.

"Did you want to say something?" she asked in her best university administration voice.

"Well," Maggie giggled, then instantly grew somber. "I think we're going to be stuck here for a while and I do mean stuck. You don't know me. Of course, you couldn't. And I don't know you either. I'm not your crazy aunt you got to be nice to and you're not my liberated and obnoxious but very bright niece. I run a restaurant. You're my customer—well, not so far, but I'm looking forward to that golden moment. But as long as this is *my* restaurant, we're going to be civil to each other—'cause I say so. And hon, I was grown up and *on my own* long before you got liberated!"

Sarah looked at her, started to contest Maggie's words, then stopped. "I'll bet you were, Ms. Day . . . I'll bet you were."

Maggie smiled. Okay. Now they could start over. But before she could say another word, a flash of movement outside caught her eye.

CHAPTER 7

The Circle Closes

ZECH YOUNG ENTERED HOLLY DAY'S talking non-stop, his hands pounding the air, his fingers twitching, recounting for the tenth time how he swerved his trusty Cadillac from the oncoming sports car.

"I tell you, it was a miracle! One minute she's right in my path— certain death—then boom," he clapped his hands, "I turn this way and that and we're off safely to the side! It was a miracle!" His voice trailed off as his looked around to see where he was. His teeth started chattering as his body caught up with the adrenalin rushing from his adventure. He had talked the whole way from the expressway. Liz had driven and Marie Thomas, her car discarded like a Matchbox toy, had ridden silently in the back seat.

"What's this?" he started up again. "What's this? I practically give up my life and I'm driven to a joint like this! We should've kept going up the road!" A full moment of silence passed before Zech Young realized that his latest judgment had been heard by all present. His lips continued to move but no words were emitted. The silence remained as Liz turned toward those gathered and merely shrugged. It was a shrug that relayed a lifetime of toleration. The man was hopeless.

"I don't care," he responded to her unspoken approbation, "I would have driven up the road."

"Hush, old man. I can hear you. Everyone's heard you! You're talking too loud."

"I'll say you are." Maggie was surprised by the entrance of her rambling guest, but not enough to lose her edge. "I take it this is another installment in the Holly Day's fan club?"

"Our car spun out—almost wrecked . . . it was a miracle . . ."

"I heard," Maggie interrupted. "So you're stuck in this 'joint' until the storm stops. Well, Merry Christmas to you, too!"

"And a Happy New Year!" Zech grumbled. "Have you got a phone?" Before Maggie could answer, Zech started in the wrong direction.

"The bathrooms are down there. Try over there," Maggie called after him. Zech turned as Maggie pointed in the opposite direction. Liz merely shrugged again. Hopeless. She pulled out a chair and plopped down. Lanny Hargrave remained immutable, sipping his coffee, watching, always watching life go on around him. Sarah and Julie retreated to a corner of the cafe, Sarah accepting a cup of coffee from Maggie, Julie accepting a cookie. Zech started pumping quarters into the pay phone. He paused, tapped the wall, stared about, then launched into an eccentric harangue with the operator whose recorded voice told him to try again.

Maggie noticed the well-dressed girl standing behind Liz and nodded toward her.

"This your daughter? Granddaughter?"

Liz puzzled over the question for an instant as thoughts of her own daughter raced through her head. Then she followed Maggie's glance and turned to the young girl behind her.

"Oh. Oh, yes. I mean, no. She was following behind us on the highway. She spun past us during the pileup and we gave her a ride."

Maggie sized up her three newest patrons and took pity. Not a friendly guest had entered yet, but they were all hapless enough. "I'm beginning to feel like the damned Christian, Kentucky, Welcome Wagon, but my name's Day and this is my place."

"I saw the name on the sign out there. You must be Holly?"

Maggie faltered. "No. Name's Maggie. What's yours?"

"I'm Liz Young. My charming husband, Zech, is on the phone."

"Real diplomat, eh?" Maggie knew Liz would understand the gibe. "And the young lady?"

The girl ignored her at first, then shivered once and seemed to come around. "My name's Marie Thomas." Her voice was haughty, full of condescension. "I'm from Chicago," she added as if that would explain everything.

"Oh," Maggie raised her eyes in mock awe, "*the* Chicago Thomases?"

"Yes, exactly," Marie noted without missing a beat.

"Never heard of them," Maggie smiled.

Marie ignored her last quip. "What kind of place is this?"

Maggie paused. The tone of the girl's voice, the quality of the fur she clutched about her, the cut of her hair, the way her eyes darted about the paneled walls of the old café, passing judgment on its decor and its inhabitants. There was much not to like about this Marie Thomas. She wore her snobbery like a cloak, covering her head to toe and defining everything about her speech, her manners, her attitudes. Maggie sensed it in an instant. She wanted to send her out with a simple, "If you don't like it, you can leave," but it was Christmas. That might not mean much, but it was enough for Maggie to give the little rich girl a break.

"Honey, this is a joint, just like Mr. Zech over there said. An old-fashioned, two-star, plain-but-simple hash house. It ain't much, and to tell you the truth it closed yesterday, but when my mom and dad started it a zillion years ago it was the only place for soldier boys and truck drivers and even folks like you to eat and rest."

Marie barely registered a response. If Maggie was getting through, Marie wasn't letting on. She looked around again. "It doesn't look like much has changed in forty years."

"You're right there. Except thirty years ago it all went to sleep."

"Are you making a joke?" Marie asked without affectation.

"The joke was on us, I guess. Progress bypassed Christian . . . and Holly Day's." Maggie was tired of talking about the past. It was about to die and she wasn't interested in postmortems. "Look folks, take off those coats, get dry, and I'll get you all some coffee."

"I don't drink coffee," Marie noted simply.

"You know, I could have guessed. I'll tell you what, I'll fix you up a nice hot cup of water."

The door flew open and Will Joseph felt his way across the threshold, his view blocked by a box of food and supplies. Maggie rushed from behind her counter refuge to help him.

"Over here, hon, over here." She guided the box to the first table near the door. Will set it down and found himself eye to eye with Marie. His jaw dropped. His eyes widened slightly. His mind closed out everything but Marie's good looks. He stared at her in awe; Maggie caught the look and her mind raced. She knew what he was thinking and she wished he wasn't. Not about Ms. Marie Thomas of Chicago! She wanted Will to experience life outside of Christian, but Marie Thomas was too much too soon. Besides,

Marie would manage to hurt him before he realized what was happening.

"Will, these folks managed to lose their way and wind up at Holly Day's!"

He simply nodded, entranced with Marie.

"Will!"

"Yes . . . yes, Maggie."

For an instant she stared at him. She wished that she could whisk him away from the premises of Holly Day's Café. She wished that she could take back her earlier admonition for Will to call her Maggie. As Miss Day she was the boss, more than an adult, someone who could steer him clear of types like Marie Thomas. As Maggie she was just another adult. Maggie had never played the role of parent, but she suddenly felt a parent's concern. If it had never snowed, the day would be half spent and Holly Day's would be drifting quietly into obscurity. Will would be with his aunt and uncle by now, celebrating Christmas. Life was full of ifs.

"Will, do me a favor and take the groceries back to the kitchen, then see if these folks need anything else. I'm going to start taking orders."

Maggie walked to where Sarah and Julie had established a corner to themselves. Julie was playing with her Barbie; Sarah looked as if she might break out in tears of frustration.

"Can I get you something to eat now . . . not a full menu, but we've got some hamburgers and milk and . . ."

"Is that old man going to finish on the phone or not!" Sarah burst out.

"Look, lady, it's a pay phone. Go tap him on the shoulder or slug him or something."

"If I don't get ahold of her father we'll never make connections!"

"So grab the damned phone from him!" Maggie's own, strained patience was reaching its limits. "Sorry, honey. I get a little ornery sometimes!"

"If he doesn't get off soon I *will* grab it! If I'm not in Cincinnati by this evening at the latest . . ."

"Yes, that's Zech . . . Z-E-C-H. Young . . . as if that matters!" Zech's voice boomed across the old dining hall.

"Good luck!" Maggie laughed. Sarah didn't join her.

"Sorry for the noise," Liz leaned over from her table and spoke in a hushed tone. "Zech's just busy making friends with the fine people at the telephone company. He's a little deaf."

"Don't worry about it, hon." Maggie flipped her hand in Zech's direction. "I've handled a lot worse on some late Saturday nights! He gives the place color!"

"The place doesn't need any more color," Sarah muttered under her breath.

"The lady said *he's* deaf . . . not me. I'm just feisty." Maggie leaned her face into Sarah's and the younger woman slunk down. "But I agree with you! The place has gotten as lively as it needs to get!"

"Well, try again!" Zech's voice again predominated the room. "He's got to be in. He's in the shower or the basement or something. I tell you . . ." Zech's voice grew more shrill and higher pitched with every syllable.

Maggie turned to Liz. "What's got him all worked up?"

"Telephones are his downfall. With phones people can simply disconnect him. You see, for Zech, everything has to happen *now*. That was what finally made him turn the jewelry stores over to Stanley."

"Jewelry stores! Are you Zech's Jewelry and Pawn Shop?"

"We *were*. I used to think getting out of the business would save his life. That was ten years ago. Now, I think it's killing him! You can never tell."

"You had a nice little store in Bowling Green."

"We had three nice little stores in all."

"I bought myself an engagement ring at Zech's—some time back." Maggie winked. "Things didn't work out. Had to take it back." Liz nodded. Maggie might have to fight with the rest of her new patrons but she had a friend in Liz Young. "So what happened to Zech?"

"Six days a week he traveled from one store to another. Seven in the morning until seven at night. Fifty-some years. He gave his all to every store. Too much. Zech turned seventy and caput . . . the whole works went . . . heart, prostate, circulation!"

"So he retired?"

"Right. But signing over the business to the kids is no retirement. He frets and worries and picks at Stanley, and now Stanley and his sister are fighting over what little's left! Discount stores killed us these past few years."

"So you're coming back from Florida for a nice little holiday of worrying about the business and the kids?"

"You got it!" Liz looked lovingly toward her aging bull. "Besides, the sunny beaches were beginning to drive him nuts. Too much roller blading and deep sea fishing and blue hair!"

"Look, I've got to use that phone." Sarah stood up. Her attempts to reach Julie's father had evolved from a simple need to a crisis.

More than that, it was a matter of principle. Zech was hogging it. "You run this place. Can't you get him to give it up?"

Maggie's jaw set with Sarah's interruption and her orders. She kicked her foot up against the bottom of the counter and tried to hold her tongue. Sarah Herald had an attitude. Of course, she did too, but at least she admitted it. And she didn't blame the world for her problems—most of the time. But Sarah was a different bird all together. "Do this—do that." "He this—he that." "They shouldn't do this—they shouldn't do that." Maggie caught herself in the midst of mentally dissecting Sarah's personality. She chuckled. Disliking Sarah wouldn't solve anything. As a matter of fact, she didn't care much what happened to Sarah. But Julie was a different matter. She wanted to help Julie. She liked the little girl. She deserved a good Christmas.

"Okay," Maggie murmured as if in afterthought, "I'll do what I can." She threw her dish towel over her shoulder and approached Zech. He saw her coming and waved her away. She continued to come and he turned his back on her. She touched him on the shoulder and he jerked around.

"Leave me alone!" he barked. "I'm paying for this phone call." To Maggie he looked as if he was on permanent hold.

They were beginning to get her down. The whole damned bunch of them. The sharp-tongued Sarah and her daughter, the bickering Youngs, the little rich snob Marie—she could do without the lot. And now, on a mission for Sarah, she was being berated by some old man. She should have taken care of Holly Day's the day before.

"Look, Mr. Young," she began again, "if you'd ease up a little bit you might find an operator who would help you get through."

"I said leave me alone! This is an important phone call! You have no right to interrupt!" The old man looked as if he might hit her.

Maggie was about to lose it all and wrap the phone cord around his throat when the front door banged open louder than it had all day. The wind spit snowflakes and ice slivers ten feet into the café. Its cold sent Marie Thomas into a fur ball and Lanny Hargrave into the retreat of his corner booth. Maggie turned and stared. Zech Young lowered the receiver from his ear.

"You suppose we could come in and warm up?" The man had a red-gray beard and dancing eyes and he was leading a young couple and their baby. He was a stranger, yet Maggie felt like she knew him. She couldn't place his face, but it was familiar. Really familiar. He looked like a truck driver. Most teamsters knew about Maggie and her café. That must be it.

"Join the party. I haven't had a crowd like this in twenty years, bud! Guess I oughta pray for snow more often!"

The broad-shouldered man leaned his head back and roared. Zech Young looked first at Maggie, then at the man he recognized from the rest stop. At least he seemed like the same man. He hadn't been laughing before.

"Who are you?" Zech's question was more an accusation.

"*Shalom!*" the big man chuckled. Zech tried but couldn't hold back a smile. "Don't you remember me from the rest stop?" the truck driver persisted.

Zech hung up the receiver. "You're acting a little differently, but I remember you." The cadence of his voice evened out. "I remember. I remember. You were in front of us when we went off the road."

"I'd rather you remember me from the rest stop than from the trouble I caused!" the man laughed. "My name's Leo. Leo DeAngelis. And this is Becky Masters and her husband, Jake, and their baby, little Jake. They wound up right behind my rig when we stopped sliding. We've gotten acquainted out there in Antarctica!"

"Well," Zech took a step away from the phone, "I'm glad you made it safe and sound."

"Thanks. I really do feel bad about you all being stuck like this. We wouldn't be here if I hadn't lost it on that soft turn."

Zech nodded in agreement at first, then mumbled, "No problem, could've been any of us," and returned to what was fast becoming his personal phone.

Leo turned to Maggie and winked. "So what's cooking, Holly?" The Masters went for hot coffee. Maggie didn't try to serve them. She was too busy staring at Leo, convinced that some night long past she might have gotten friendly with this guy. There was a presence about him that filled the room, a familiarity that made her want to stay around him. Maybe she had fallen for him sometime way back. Besides, he was the first of her new patrons who acted half pleased to have a place to eat and rest. The first welcome guest to cross her threshold.

"Cooking?" she repeated, as if the word had been spoken in Greek. "We're just having a dandy time!" Her voice dropped. "But the name's Maggie."

"Maggie, oh . . . well, sorry about that. It's been a while." Leo's half-smile made Maggie turn away for a second. There was something about him that threw her off. His familiarity was engaging, but also startling. "What's his problem?" Leo nodded toward Zech.

"He's been trying to get through to his son for almost an hour. Phones are all tied up."

"Maybe I can help."

"I wouldn't if I were you. He's kinda like a dog with his food."

"Let's see."

Maggie watched as the newcomer walked over to the telephone. Zech wasn't talking, only holding the receiver again. As he saw Leo approach he brought it closer to his chest.

"Can I borrow that for a minute, friend?"

"I'm calling my son."

"Doesn't look like you're calling anybody right now."

"Well, I will be. I've got it . . ."

Leo reached over and gently slipped the receiver from Zech's grasp. "Not anymore. Now step aside for a second."

Zech complied. Leo smiled. "What number are you trying to call?"

Zech gave Leo the number, awed by anyone who would challenge him. Leo turned and spun his fingers about the old rotary dial. He cupped his hand over the mouthpiece and turned to Zech.

"Must have been the way you were dialing it. It's ringing now." Leo handed the receiver back to Zech.

Zech brought it to his ear and listened. The ringing stopped. Someone was picking up. "Stanley . . ." Zech practically shouted his son's name. "Yes . . . we're safe. We're all stuck for a while, but we're safe. Okay, I'll give you the number . . ."

Zech's voice became more civil and less brusque as Leo walked back to Maggie.

"Now we can have fun, eh?" Leo said.

Maggie laughed. "At least I won't kill him!"

Leo smiled. Maggie's face squinched up as she tried to remember. She scratched her hair, then shook her head as if trying to free up old memories. Where had she seen him? She was too embarrassed to ask. It would come to her.

"It could stand to be a little warmer in here." Leo's breath turned into a cloud.

"Well, if some people didn't bring in the cold air, it wouldn't be so bad!" Maggie wisecracked.

"Fair enough!" he grinned. "But it's still cold in here. Got a problem with the heater?"

"Yeah, it's five degrees out there and about forty in here!"

"It's your fuel oil, isn't it? You're almost out."

Maggie's face paled. He was right. She had avoided fueling up before she closed. Too much money wasted on a place with no future. The prospect of arctic temperatures had frightened her that morning. Now it was frightening her more with the prospect of keeping her pilgrims alive through the night. She couldn't remain silent any longer. A lie was the next best thing.

"Tanker truck's just a call away, rain or shine!"

"Rain or shine, maybe, but not in a blizzard," Leo exhorted. "If we don't get working on it, we won't have any heat by nightfall. Listen to that sputtering." In the silence that followed everyone noticed for the first time the slight hissing and popping in the several gas space heaters spread around the café.

"Any suggestions?" Maggie hated meddlers without answers.

"Let's get the old wood stove stoked up."

"It don't work."

"There's not a whole lot to go wrong in a wood stove—s'posing you're careful not to start a place on fire."

"Yeah, except this one *don't work*. Boy, you all are all alike! Is anyone gonna take my word on something?"

"I can get it going for you. Just lend me Mr. Will Joseph here and I'll bet we can get it roaring in no time!"

"It don't work, I tell you. And I don't want you starting fires in that old piece of junk."

"Just turn the other way and don't look. Besides, I don't think we got much choice."

"It's broke and that's final."

"We'll get it crackling and that's final!" Leo laughed.

"That'll be the day."

"What'll you bet me?"

"A square meal and a warm bed," she said.

"Meal, maybe, but nobody's goin' to see a warm bed tonight. How 'bout we bet for a Christmas present?"

"And what Christmas present would that be?"

"We'll know when the time comes."

She started to retort, then her fury faded like winds in a sail. Leo was smiling at her and she felt just like mush. How was she going to stop the big hulk if he wanted to do something?

CHAPTER 8

Leo and His Charges

MAGGIE STOOD BY THE COUNTER as Leo recruited one guest after another for his stove project. She smiled, trying not to be smug, shifting her dish towel from her right shoulder to her left, wiping down the counter for a third time, looking busy even when she wasn't. There was no use telling him the old iron maiden wouldn't work, or that it might even blow up in his face—he was the type who wouldn't listen.

Not that she didn't want the stove to work—at least for the moment. It just didn't. Besides, she didn't like people taking over. Well, not taking over exactly, but getting things done. Getting things done in her place! It was bad enough that the pilgrims griped so much. But she could stand that. She was still in control. They could complain all they wanted. But now Leo was leading a damned revolt! Mobilizing the troops and taking over the place. Not by a long shot, she thought. It wasn't much of a place, but it was her place.

Maggie was convinced that she was no more a loner than anyone else in the nineties. The world was a different place from what it was when she was a girl. More realistic, less idealistic. That's just the way things were. Things change and that's that.

Then, in walks Mr. Good Old Boy talking about starting up the old stove and organizing everyone like some socialist. He'd fall on his face. She was sure of it. She understood all too well the pain of trying to get people to work together. Just when you thought you could get somewhere as a team, someone would decide he had a better way, then someone else would decide that way wasn't so good, and in a little while the team wasn't a team anymore. She remembered all of the times she'd tried to get the merchants of Christian to save their little downtown. They hadn't listened. Maggie's face soured with the recollection of her failures.

"Will, have ya got a screwdriver and a hammer?" Leo asked.

"Yes, sir."

"Well, go get 'em, and some newspaper and some kindling."

"Yes, sir."

"And a few pieces of that wood lying out on the side over there."

"Now look, friend." Maggie sauntered over to where Leo had begun examining the damper. She was tired of his cheery blabber. The man was outwearing his welcome. "That old firetrap doesn't work."

"It'll work . . . Maggie."

"I've had it looked at and they told me to scrap it!"

"You got bad advice." Leo continued puttering, never once looking at her. "It's all clogged up—could cause a fire if you weren't careful, but it'll work."

Maggie folded her arms and huffed, looking around for support. There was none. She wasn't being ignored, just overridden. She would have preferred being ignored. She slowly clenched her fists, her anger growing again. Will returned with the hammer and screwdriver. Leo took them and started loosening the various sections of stovepipe.

"What are you trying . . . to make a liar out of me?" Her voice had lost its cynicism, her smirk settling into a sneer.

"Just trying to get a little warmth in this place of yours." Leo's voice sounded muffled and far away, his face stuck through the door of the stove.

"We got plenty of LP fuel and *no wood* to burn, Mr. Know It All!"

Leo removed his face from the stove door. He leaned toward her and spoke, his voice softer than a baby's chin. "You're running low on LP—that's why it keeps sputtering—and there's wood over on the side of the house." His smile turned into a grin as Will Joseph stumbled through the front door, his arms filled with short limbs. He dropped his load beside the stove, snow and ice bouncing off the logs and flying in every direction.

Maggie was caught without a come back. She could have sworn the wood pile had gone to rot years before. "Okay," was all that she could muster, then, "it's a firetrap! Don't say I didn't tell you!"

Leo winked, returned to his work, then looked up again. "We're going to get it working . . . and it's *not* going to cause any fires."

Maggie retreated to her counter. The stranger was reading her mind. She could tell by the gleam in his eye and the slight bit of sarcasm meant only for her ears. Not that her thoughts were all that tough to read. When a place wasn't worth anything more than its insurance, then it was time to sell it to the insurance company. Will might not know about such things, but an old truck driver like Leo would. The creepy thing was having him hint around, making you wonder if he knew your plans. It just wasn't any of his business and that was that. And still he made it his business.

He was a big old self-confident, swaggering truck jockey. Just like most of the men she had served steaks to by the pound and mashed potatoes by the scoop. They hadn't been around for years. She missed them. She missed their company and she missed their money, but she had forgotten that they were so cocksure of themselves. That she didn't miss. Or did she? Maggie wondered. She had never let it bother her before, why should she let it bother her now?

She watched him work with the damper until it opened and shut; then he closed the fuel door and banged on the old stovepipe. A slight cloud of black puffed from around gaps in the door. Then Leo got on a chair and tapped farther up the pipe until he reached a point just before it exited the inner wall.

"Just like I figgered," he said to himself.

"What is it?" Will stood by his side. Maggie's face turned crimson. She was jealous of the attention the man was getting.

"All the creosote stuck on this bend—trapped the soot until it shut down the draw."

It sounded reasonable to Maggie. Maybe he knew what he was talking about. But it still wasn't burning wood.

Leo worked his way around the elbow joint and the black cloud around the door darkened. The thud of little clinkers on the bed of old ash made Will turn to Maggie and nod. Her eyes narrowed and she pursed her lips. It wasn't working yet. Then she looked at the others in the room. They were all watching and everyone started nodding as if to say, "Now we're getting somewhere."

Maggie's eyes roamed from one to another. She could read their thoughts and feelings. Zech Young stopped his incessant pacing by the telephone, waiting for Stanley to call back. Instead, he walked over to Leo and stood next to Will, trying to think of something to say, some advice he might offer. Maggie realized that she might have the power to contain an old salesman like Zech Young, but so far she hadn't had much luck at distracting him. Leo had.

Liz Young relaxed for the first time since she had walked into Holly Day's. Maggie knew enough about people to realize that Liz had more common sense and wisdom than Zech ever had. Yet for their entire marriage she had probably made Zech feel like he was always making the major decisions. She had nurtured Zech like a child and now she seemed all too glad to give him over to Leo for a while.

Marie Thomas loosened her grip on her fur and scooted her chair forward to watch, her mind finally on something other than herself. Maggie noticed for the first time that when Marie let her guard down she looked ten years younger. She couldn't be much older than Will, maybe younger. Something was bothering the girl. No one with that much money and good looks could be that aloof unless she had something on her mind.

Sarah stopped gritting her teeth. Maggie didn't have to know her life story to realize that Sarah was still angry at Julie's father. Whatever he'd done—besides separation and divorce—couldn't be worth the bitterness Sarah had borne him for some time. Maggie knew all about broken promises, but she hated dwelling on them and she hated hearing other people who did. Now Sarah looked halfway human as she watched Leo. Sarah the efficiency machine, Sarah the leader of the movement, Sarah the woman standing alone against all odds seemed to fade away as Sarah the human being emerged.

Julie began stacking small pieces of wood by the stove in neat piles. The way she did it, it looked like play. Maggie's heart went out to her. Christmas Eve afternoon and no toys, no father to meet her, no friends with whom to play. The kid must be bored stiff. Maggie didn't blame her for jumping to the task. She might resent the truck driver, but he sure had a knack for getting people interested in what he was doing.

Even Jake and Becky Masters seemed more relaxed. Of all the newcomers, these two and their baby were folks who could have been from Christian or anywhere close by. And Maggie guessed they were the ones who had the most to worry about. They were folks she could talk to with no problem. Maggie dropped her towel on the counter and slipped over next to Becky.

"Is he teething yet?" Maggie asked.

"Just started. He's been fussy ever since."

"Can I hold him?" Maggie could hardly believe what she was doing, but Becky looked like she needed a moment's rest and, for one reason or another, Jake seemed distracted. Becky smiled and yielded the child over. Maggie nestled him in her arms and made faces at him. Little Jake looked up and giggled.

"What brings you all out in weather like this?" Maggie asked casually.

"If I get to E-town by Christmas I've got a job," Jake answered without looking at her.

"This economy's got us all behind," Maggie didn't know what else to say, "but you look like a determined fellow, Mr. Masters. I'll lay odds you get a job real soon."

"That's what I've been telling him, ma'am . . ." Becky echoed.

"Just call me Maggie."

Becky smiled. She needed a friend and it made Maggie feel good to be there.

"This isn't the first job I've chased after," Jake added.

"I think you'll do okay, Mr. Masters. I just got a feelin'." Maggie wasn't as sure as she sounded, but she couldn't see the harm of putting on the act.

Jake Masters slowly grinned. "My name's Jake," he said. "As long as we're on first names."

"That's a deal," Maggie said.

Maggie patted the baby and joined the Masters in watching Leo. If nothing else, the trucker's tinkering had focused their attention on something besides their predicament. The absence of Zech's and Sarah's grousing alone brought relief from the tension that had built up in their Christmas prison. And it was good to see the rich girl from Chicago loosen up a little. Not much, but a little.

Leo finished his tapping. The rattling sounds ceased and he turned to his new disciples. "Well, folks, let's fire her up!"

He stepped down from the chair with a loud grunt and got back down on his knees. "Paper, Will." Will started crumpling up newspaper and Leo put it in the stove. "Julie, how about some of those little twigs and sticks you've been stacking so well?" Julie gathered up a handful and moved expectantly to Leo's side. He added the sticks to the bed of newspaper in a crisscross fashion and leaned back. "Zech, you gotta match?"

The old man started fumbling through his coat and pants pockets. His bushy eyebrows raised as he found a packet of motel matches tangled among his change and keys. He withdrew his hand and presented the matches to Leo as if he were offering some great gift. "I got 'em! I got 'em right here."

"Great!" Leo clapped his hands together. "Now step back everybody. This old stove might blow yet!"

"I'd be willing to bet on it!" Maggie's sarcasm was matched only by the eagerness she shared with the others. She alone in the room could remember what nights and long winter days had been like when the stove's warmth had spread over the room filled with travelers.

At first the newspaper looked as if it would smother the flame rather than feed it. Yellow light played across the top of the paper, barely tickling the twigs and bigger pieces of wood. Leo got down on his knees and blew on the feeble light. A few seconds passed and the flame began to grow. Maggie waited for the smoke. The last several times she'd fired it up—ten, almost fifteen years before—there had been great billows curling out from the bed of kindling. She waited, then inched forward, and finally dropped her jaw in amazement. There was a fire in there; not a big one, but a fire all the same. The kindling had caught. Leo eased a larger branch into the stove and the fire jumped up an inch or two. Then he closed the door and turned to Zech.

"Zech, you suppose you could keep the fire going for us?" Leo made it sound more like an honor than a chore.

"Fire? Can I keep a fire going, mister? Well, I should say I can keep a fire going."

"Zech, just tell the man you'll watch the fire," Liz scolded.

"I'll watch the fire, I'll watch the fire!" he retorted.

"Jake."

"Yeah."

"Could you manage the wood pile—keep a good supply drying off here next to the stove?"

"Well, sure. I can do that. Sure." Jake Masters straightened up. He had been slump-shouldered since walking into the restaurant.

"Now, Maggie . . ." Leo paused. Their eyes met. She knew he had something in mind. It was still her place. She didn't have to let this guy take over.

"What?"

"Suppose we could get something hot and tasty cooking back in the kitchen?"

Sarah entered the exchange before Maggie could answer. "Wood piles for the men folks, kitchen duty for the women?"

Maggie waited to see what Leo would say. The truck driver only smiled.

"Ma'am, I'd be glad to cook, but it would be the ruin of good food!"

"Honey," Maggie laid her hand on Sarah's shoulder, "I hate to tell you, but I run this joint and I'm the only cook we got. And cooking *is* my business. But I appreciate the sisterly concern."

"Maybe Sarah's got a point, though," Leo interceded, smiling. "After all, this is a *closed* joint—you don't run it anymore."

"Listen, buster, it's still my place!"

"I thought those Nashville folks bought it," he said.

Maggie drew back. It was none of his business. Will must have been telling things out of turn while they were working on the stove.

"That's none of your worry. Today and tonight this place is mine."

"Still, Sarah's right. We're all right. If you'll get us a meal going, I'll recruit the cleanup crew. Fair enough?"

"Fair enough!" Will offered.

"I could clean this place up so that you'd never recognize it!" Zech Young finished poking the last small log that he had added to the stove's growing inferno.

"I can cook spaghetti!" Julie dusted her hands clean of kindling bark.

"Jake says my soup's the best in seven counties," Becky spoke in her soft, near whisper of a voice.

"Then let's get it going, Maggie!" Leo ended the discussion.

Everyone in the room dispersed to their tasks. There wasn't that much to do. It wasn't very hard. But it would keep them busy for a while, and for the first time since they had wandered into Holly Day's Café, Maggie's pilgrims stopped thinking about themselves and started thinking about each other and the rest of the evening. Maggie was dumbfounded, even as she caught herself being absorbed into Leo's zeal. Almost like the old days. Everyone found something to do—everyone, that is, except Marie. Caught in her own melodrama, she could only look out the window and wonder what it would be like to become part of the countryside. In a while it would be dark.

❄ ❄ ❄ ❄ ❄ ❄ ❄ ❄ ❄ ❄

Christmas songs were still pouring forth from WCHR when Maggie started getting out dishes and mugs for dinner. She hummed along with Bing and Perry and Nat Cole and even Frank Sinatra, singing the words when she could remember them.

She was mid-verse with Frank, singing "I'll Be Home for Christmas," when a loud crack outside silenced everyone but Sinatra. A slower, rending squeal followed as the biggest limb on Holly's giant oak twisted and crashed toward the ground. There was another pop as the splitting wood downed an electrical line. No radio. No lights.

Maggie threw her towel down and rushed to the window. Outside, a utility pole tipped over, slowly at first, then building momentum until it landed on top of two snow-covered cars. They collapsed like squished donuts as the main supply wire fell to the ground. It started dancing and jumping like a snake on fire. Everything happened in a few seconds, but the wire continued to dance and strut about the road even after the crashing and cracking ended. It singed holes in the snow and lurched from side to side.

Maggie was the only one to move; the rest froze in place. Dishes seemed suspended in midair. Zech held a log half in and half out of the wood stove. Then, drawn by the dancing cable, everyone moved to the bank of front windows, watching it jerk and jump from one spot to another. Its effect was hypnotic. No one spoke, no one watched anything but the jumping cable. No one moved. No one except Julie.

As the limb fell, Julie was standing just inside the door, her boots and coat on to go out for small pieces of wood. She'd been doing it for an hour and the adults had lost track of her. Even Sarah had let Julie go about as she pleased. Now distracted by the sudden darkness and the spectacle of the power line, Sarah didn't notice as Julie slowly opened the door. So slowly that the bell barely jiggled.

When the tree and pole came crashing down, Julie forgot about gathering wood. She wanted to see the dancing cable close up. She wondered what made it hop up and down. She wondered if it would stop hopping if she grabbed it. She didn't run to it. She didn't make any noise. She stalked the downed power line and it was the deliberation of her movements that kept everyone from noticing her until she was only a few feet from it.

Zech was the first to take his eyes from the wire itself. Still obsessed with the telephone, he realized that the limb that had cut off their power may have also snapped the phone line. He started for the phone to check it out and saw Julie already out the door. He struggled to call Julie's name, forgot it for a moment, and cried out, "Quick!" in frustration. They all turned. Sarah screamed Julie's name, but most of the sound caught in her throat. Maggie and Will broke for the door. Jake Masters was there before them, throwing the door open and slogging through the snowdrifts like a man caught in a dream. The rest of Holly Day's patrons, like so many pinballs gone awry, collided with each other, the tables, and the chairs.

While they stumbled toward the door or pounded at the windows, Julie skimmed across the crusted snow, the dancing cable slithering inches from her feet. Like a wonderful toy, it snapped right and left, begging her to touch it, just once, for fun.

"No!" Maggie found her voice and it sounded like a bullhorn. To Julie it was only a whisper, but it made her stop for a millisecond.

Leo's hulking frame appeared from the side of the restaurant and in one sweeping motion he grabbed Julie up in his arms and stumbled backwards in the snow. Maggie collapsed in a chair. Sarah found her legs and rushed outside.

"Did you see that?" Will's question was to everyone and no one.

"Where the hell was he?" Jake pointed toward Leo. He thought he had been the only one to make it outside.

Leo carried Julie back inside; she was more embarrassed than frightened, unaware of what had nearly happened. Sarah grabbed her as soon as she could reach Leo's extended arms. Leo looked over at Jake and Will.

"I was by the wood pile. I didn't know she was behind me. I guess we got lucky."

"You can say that again!" Maggie sighed. She stood up and moved toward the front door. "I could've sworn we were all in here when the lights went out!"

"My fault." Leo hung his head. "I must have left the door open a crack when I went out. Damned branch nearly got me as it fell." He pointed to the tree bent low with snow and ice.

Maggie scratched her head. "You weren't right next to me at the counter?"

"Right before I went out, sure . . ."

"You're a hero!" Zech proclaimed. "You saved her life!"

"That's for sure," Will added to the chorus.

"Thank Miss Day," Leo said. "I was still wading through snow when she cried out. That little girl stopped just long enough for me to snatch her."

Maggie shook her head. "Well I hardly think . . ."

"No . . . no . . ." Zech silenced Maggie with a wave of his hand. "He's right. We all stood like bumps . . . you're the one that took charge." He looked toward the phone, still intent on his hook-up to Stanley. "I'd better check if the lines are still working."

In an instant he cried back. "No. They're down too."

Maggie felt a shiver cross her shoulders. They needed light and they needed the phone. It may have been Zech and Sarah's plaything, but for everyone else it was a safety net. Now it was gone. The wood stove was their only source of heat or light and the chance of Buddy Wendell's return was their only hope of a link with outside help. Neither was very reassuring. She folded her arms and paced the room for a second, then turned to Will.

"I got some of Mom's old kerosene lamps in the shed out back. Give me a hand and we'll go get 'em." Will started back with her.

"I'll help," Leo said.

"Fine. You can grab the kerosene. I got a five-gallon drum of it."

"Kerosene's always handy to have around," Leo said.

There he goes again, Maggie thought, making little wisecracks that sound like something but don't amount to anything.

"I use it for the lamps."

"If it's more than a year old it might be bad." Leo's tone was matter-of-fact.

"It's fresh enough," Maggie barked.

"I guess it is," Leo smiled. "I guess it is," he repeated to himself.

Maggie looked at him, trying to figure out what he knew and what he thought he knew. Just when she was warming up to him, he started prying into areas that were none of his business.

CHAPTER 9

On Christmas Eve

THE ENDLESS, GRAY AFTERNOON faded into Christmas Eve. The only light inside the café came from the kerosene lamps and the wood stove. As daylight ended, it grew colder. The colder it got, the more Maggie realized that Julie's wasn't the only life Leo had saved. The last sputtering pops of LP gas came with dinner. The flames on the cook stove died and Jake pitched more wood into the potbelly.

Leo had been right, Maggie wrong, and Maggie resented it more than ever. She retreated behind the counter, chafing at her own stupidity, feeling used and lost in her own place. He had saved their lives. That was for sure. Heat was life in weather like this. Maybe the others hadn't known about people freezing to death, but Maggie had.

Every few years they found one of Christian's seniors stiff as a block. Buddy Wendell would tell her all about it over coffee. "Not bad if you gotta go," he had ruminated. "You can never tell if they're forgetful, or too cheap or too proud to take county aid. Maybe they're just ready to give up." Maggie had listened and poured him another cup of coffee. Now she remembered his stories as she sipped coffee heated on the cast iron top of the old wood stove. Buddy said they all seemed to go pretty peacefully.

Maggie shuddered. Even with the wood stove it couldn't be

73

more than fifty degrees inside the café. That was better than ten degrees below outside, but it would start to trouble them as the night wore on, especially Zech and his wife. It would have troubled them a lot more if Leo hadn't figured a way to fire the old stove up. Leo again. So maybe he saved them. She didn't have to like it and she didn't have to treat him like her boss. It was still her café even if no one wanted to be there. She couldn't blame them. But she called the shots, not some bearded teamster.

Maggie stared outside. Dry, icy flakes spun in little cyclones. Drifts were nearing four feet. John's Grocery had closed hours before the power failed. Holly Day's might be on Main Street, but it looked like the only outpost for a million miles.

She was trapped in her own place. Ownership only meant it was hers again when they all left. And when they all left she'd have nothing but worthless square footage on Main Street in Christian. It wasn't like it was supposed to be. Her wishes weren't being followed and her desires weren't being met.

Maggie's thoughts raced over the past thirty years. Sunoco had tried to buy the café twenty years before. Then some outlet mall—she and John and the other merchants had fought that too. But why? Nothing had ever come of the restaurant once the interstate was opened. No high-minded preservationists had ever shown any interest in downtown Christian. For years she'd fought to keep the place until it could come back. Why or how it would come back she couldn't imagine, but that was her dream. She wanted to fill the joint with voices and laughter and the smell of people. Just a few hours before she thought her dream might be coming true. Now she felt like she didn't own the place anymore. It belonged to a crabby old man and a sharp-tongued woman and a truck driver who went around solving problems. She was something less than a landlord and that wasn't enough. Sooner or later the power company would send out a repair truck and get the electricity back on. The telephone would start ringing. In a few days the LP tank truck would deliver enough fuel to keep the pipes from bursting. And the pilgrims would all be gone. But now, with nothing working right, they were all here and she felt helpless and alone.

Her charges were the problem and they were the solution; but Leo was the biggest problem of all. He could do everything she couldn't. He could keep them warm, safe . . . at peace. Maggie smiled, taking another sip of her coffee. At least he couldn't feed them.

The smell of solid food, generously spiced, hung in the air along with smoke from the wood stove. She had thrown together a good dinner. Not a Christmas feast. There wasn't any turkey or stuffing or pies or any of that stuff. But the food filled them up and it ended their hunger for a while. There was spaghetti and meat sauce, warm bread and some baked beans, canned fruit and some cheese. Everyone ate. No one complained. They all helped. With that thought, Maggie's feelings about her customers began to change.

Zech and Sarah *had* mellowed once the phone lines went out. Maggie laughed to herself. Cut 'em off from worrying and complaining and fussing at each other and the world, and they were okay. Not great company and not much fun at a party, but they were better than they had been when they popped into Holly Day's. Sarah had actually hummed a tune while she stirred the meat sauce. Not a very good tune and she wasn't much of a hummer, but it was better than listening to her gripe. Zech had continued with his stories of past retailing glories. Maggie could still hear the low rumble of his laughter as complaints about his son and daughter softened.

Maggie noticed Julie spending more and more time looking out the window, wondering if Santa Claus was going to be able to find her. Maggie wondered how her mother was going to explain that one. Would she even try? Maybe the girl's father was to blame for that too. Maggie's smile died. She thought of Will. Santa hadn't visited him since he was six. Jasper and Oma were good people, but there wasn't much fun in them. They were tough, pragmatic, hard-working types. They hadn't figured on even having a son and once Will got to school age they stopped treating him like a little boy.

The wind was picking up outside. A body couldn't last very long without a lot of cover. Even then she'd have to keep moving. If she fell down or sat down or just fell asleep she'd be gone in no time. Maggie thought again about Will and what she couldn't provide for him. She had a small policy on her life—bought it the same time she did the policy on the café. It wasn't much, but if anything happened to her it would help him along. Get him out of Christian and in school down in Nashville. He couldn't drive expensive cars like Marie of the Chicago Thomases, but he'd do all right. Even if he suspected she'd done it on purpose, he'd have to forgive her some time. He'd put the money to good use; Will was a good boy.

So maybe that was it. Walk a hundred yards in any direction and just plop down. Make it look like you went out for wood and got confused. Maggie took a deep breath and edged toward the door. She was toying with herself, like someone on the edge of a cliff, half daring herself to jump.

"Thanks for the dinner." Leo caught her off guard and she jumped. "Now, what's for dessert?"

"Good Lord, you creep up on a person!"

"No use stomping around, making a racket."

"Well, just don't . . . don't come up on me like that again."

"Go out in that weather and nobody'd be coming up on you!"

She leaned across her counter and presented him with a piece of apple pie. Then she eyed him up and down. Could he read her thoughts too? She wasn't really going to head out there. She wasn't that dumb. She was just wondering. So what was he talking about, anyway?

"Good food and hospitality." He waved his fingers from his forehead in a loose salute.

"Glad you like it." Maggie took a deep breath and started pressing her apron with the greasy palms of her hands. This guy was strange.

"Where did ya hide this?" Leo nodded toward his fork full of pie.

"I got some secret places behind this counter, Mr. DeAngelis."

"Good thing you didn't walk off anywhere . . . who'd 'a known where the pie was hid?"

"Now there you go again." He had her fidgeting and nervous.

"Just passing time. Just passing time." He looked outside for what seemed like several seconds. "You really could catch your death out there."

"Now stop it, I tell ya."

"You were thinking about a walk. You had it written all over your face."

"Now you're reading my face, eh? Can't fix it like you do a stove, can you?"

"Will would *never* understand. Never."

Her eyes narrowed and her jaw set. "Mister, I don't know who you are or how my business is your business, but I wish you'd mind your own."

"Easy now, Holly . . ."

"And the name's Maggie, understand?"

"I understand just fine."

"Good, then stop it. You hear me? I don't know what road you've been driving, but when this storm blows over I'd just as soon you were back on it!"

"I don't mean to cause you trouble."

"Well, you have! You put my guests to work, then you steal away my help . . ."

"Nobody's going to steal Will from you!"

"I didn't say that."

"But that's what you were thinking."

"Stop acting like you can read my thoughts . . . 'cause you can't!" Maggie felt like flicking out his eye with the tip of her dish towel. He'd gotten to her. Gotten to her heart and to her soul, and there wasn't much she could do about it except get mad. She was alone, her family gone, no husband, no lover. There was no one to say good night to in the evening or good morning to in the groggy dawn. No one except Will Joseph. And it sure felt like Leo was taking him away.

"These people need you . . . all of them."

"Stop it."

"Will needs you. If anything ever happened to you, he'd blame himself."

"Don't say that."

"Besides, you're the best friend he's got. And friends are a lot more important than money in the bank."

"Well, look who's talking! You probably got enough money socked away to last forever!"

"Forever's a long time."

"Right! And a wife and kids too."

"Nope. They died." He said it matter-of-factly. No anger. No remorse. No hinted request for sympathy. But the effect on Maggie was immediate. Her shoulders slumped down and her chin sagged. Was he lying to her?

"Look, I don't know anything about you. If you lost your family then I'm sorry. Awful sorry. But this is my place and I've been running it a long time. Then you pop in here on Christmas Eve like the damned Salvation Army and you start telling me how to do everything."

"I've only done things 'cause you wouldn't."

Maggie wanted to get away. Leo was prying and prodding into her business and she wouldn't tolerate that from anyone. Her eyes darted around, searching for something—anything or anyone that needed attention.

"I gotta go in the back, make sure we got more kerosene for the lamps." She nodded and started back through the kitchen.

"Don't get it confused with that gasoline back there."

"You don't miss much, do you? Did ya count how many pairs of shoes I had while you were back that way?"

"Nope," he smiled.

"Well, I guess I can tell kerosene from gasoline. Gas is in the mower can." She started back.

"But you gotta be careful," he continued, "spill one or both of them and you'll be selling the place to the insurance company instead of those video folks from Nashville."

"Look, what I sell and who I sell it to is none of your business!"

"True." He turned around while he munched at his pie and looked at the pilgrims gathered close to the wood stove for warmth. "I do think of these folks as my business . . . what with my rig's being the cause for them being here and all." He wasn't facing her as he spoke, but she heard him and had to respond.

"Well, they're not my business. 'Cause I'm closed!"

"Maybe . . . but you're doing a good job by 'em."

She walked back toward him. She was tired of his compliments and his good cheer.

"You'd do a better job without me, Mr. DeAngelis. You have so far."

"I did what I know how to do."

Maggie's attention flagged as she saw Will walking up to Marie Thomas. He had finally found his nerve. He started talking to her with his eyes turned away. Not good, she thought. Look her in the eyes. Smile. Stand up straight. Show some confidence. Don't let her think you're frightened of her.

"She might be a handful for Will." Leo interrupted her diversion.

"Hmm? Oh, yeah. Well, I don't think we've got anything long term starting up."

"Why do you think's she's off to herself so much?" he asked.

"Don't know. Just stuck up probably."

"Maybe. Maybe she's got something other than Will on her mind." Leo glanced at her out of the corner of his eye. "She's one I'd stay clear of . . . you and Will both."

Maggie felt the fire flare up in her. "I beg your pardon. I stay clear of who I want to stay clear of, understand?"

"Suit yourself."

Leo smiled and strolled away. Maggie shook her head. What a nerve! She started back for the kerosene muttering to herself about his meddlesome ways. She wasn't three steps inside the bedroom when she realized it was freezing—just like it would be in the café without the wood stove. Leo again! The man was uncanny. He bothered her all right, but not enough to really dislike him. In his own, know-it-all way he wasn't so bad. He probably meant well.

Maggie grabbed the can of kerosene and escaped the cold. No use bothering herself with Leo and his jabber. There would be chores to do all night and they begged attention. She emerged from the cold back room and shivered. She looked around as if she expected something to have changed in the moment or two she was in the back.

Marie was sitting with arms folded, staring outside as Will tried to tell her something. Maggie was embarrassed for him. She caught her breath and her heart seemed to catch. "Don't just stand there," her thoughts told him. "Stop flirting—she's not worth it." She started to call him. Anything to yank him away from her. Then he turned abruptly, walking back toward Maggie. As he passed near her, she took his arm and drew him near the counter.

"How's Miss Fur Coat and Nail Polish?"

"I don't know . . . she wouldn't tell me."

Maggie laughed. "She's pretty enough."

"I guess."

"She snub you?"

"That would've been a step up. I think in her mind she just spit on me."

"Maybe *you're* not what's on her mind."

"That's for sure, but what is?" Will shrugged.

"She's a tough read all right."

Will grinned. "So why don't you give it a try?"

Maggie remembered Leo's admonition to stay away from Marie. Why should she listen to him? "Maybe I will," she said. "Tell you what. Watch me. After we finish a little girl talk, I'll signal you if I think she's warming up."

"What signal?"

"I'll pinch my nose, like this." She brought her thumb and forefinger up to her nose and squeezed its tip.

"Good luck . . . holler if you need help."

Maggie smiled. Will believed in her. That felt good. She put her towel down slowly on the counter. Then she undid her apron and slung it to one side. Stay clear of her, she thought. "We'll show Mr. DeAngelis," she said out loud.

"What? Show him what?"

"Never mind."

Maggie slid up beside Marie much like Leo had crept up on her. One minute she wasn't there, the next minute she was. Marie gave a start and it made Maggie feel good—she wasn't the only one around her place who was jumpy, and Leo wasn't the only one who could make someone jump.

"Dinner suit you, hon?" Maggie asked.

"It was okay."

"You didn't eat much."

"I wasn't hungry." Marie paused. "Look, I'll pay for the whole meal."

"Now don't offend me, hon." Maggie held up her hand. "I wasn't worried about the tab."

"It sounded like it."

"So how long you goin' to be home for Christmas?"

"Look, I can pay the bill . . ."

"I know you can pay the bill! Now cut it out." Maggie shifted her feet and plopped her hands on her hips. "I just wanted to talk . . . thought you might want—to talk. Pass some time. Whatever."

Marie stared at Maggie, her perfect eyes growing large. "I don't even know you."

"Sometimes talking to a stranger is easier than talking to an old friend. Besides, we're all stuck here together . . ."

"You can say that again."

"I could, but I won't. The point is, we won't see each other again after tonight. And that's fine."

Marie brushed a dark lock of hair away from her brow. Her eyes were large, deep brown and they were focused on Maggie's watery, flint blues. She nodded slightly, then spoke deliberately.

"I appreciate the offer. I've got some things going on right now. I'll work them out."

"Look," Maggie saw the direct approach was getting her nowhere, "it's just that I don't get women in here very often—young or old—and when I do, I like to check out what's going on in the world."

Marie slowly relaxed. "You remind me of my great aunt."

"Thanks! At least I don't remind you of your great uncle."

Marie smiled for the first time. "She's got a lot of personality too."

"How's that?"

Marie began to talk and Maggie eased back farther in her chair. Just talking was fine. The girl looked like she needed to pass some idle time with someone. Maggie was glad to oblige.

❄ ❄ ❄ ❄ ❄ ❄ ❄ ❄ ❄ ❄

"I wouldn't worry so much about getting to Cincinnati." Leo knew that was the only thing Sarah had worried about since he saw her vying with Zech for the phone.

"And why wouldn't you?" Sarah's jaw tightened slightly.

"'Cause it won't do you any good. You might as well try to worry the snow into stopping!"

"I don't want to be rude," Sarah fixed her most imperative stare upon him, "but I don't think it's any of your business."

Leo merely smiled. He nodded toward Julie who was holding

forth to Zech and Elizabeth with great animation. "That little girl's a real corker."

"She's very bright."

"Must take after you."

Sarah should have rankled at his flattery—if that's what it was—but it felt too good. She loosened slightly. "And her father," Sarah sighed, "that's where she gets her stubborn streak."

Leo smiled again. "I see" was all he needed to say. Then he nodded toward Jake and Becky.

"They must have a healthy stubborn streak as well."

Sarah had been so busy thinking about getting out of Holly Day's, she hadn't thought about the people inside of it. "What do you mean?"

"Well, they told me coming in that Jake's set on getting to Elizabethtown. Some job's opened up or whatever."

"It won't wait till after Christmas?"

"He figured it was first-come, first-served, so they wrapped up the baby and headed up the road in their old junker. That's pretty stubborn!"

"How long's he been looking for a job?"

"About three months—so he says. I'd guess closer to six."

"How do they pay the bills?"

Leo laughed. "I guess they don't. If you want to know, ask 'em yourself."

"I don't know them."

"Well, I guess you're right there—except nobody knows anyone here tonight. You could always introduce yourself." Leo stretched and made motions to leave. "Suit yourself. I'm going to walk around."

Before she could comment, Leo was gone. She looked at Jake and Becky playing with their son. It wouldn't hurt to see if she could help Becky out in some way. She probably needed a break. She wouldn't admit it to him, but Leo was right about Cincinnati. There wasn't a thing she could do about getting there or even calling to let Julie's father know they were stuck. The least she could do was talk to the Masters. Sarah unfolded her arms, stood up, and walked toward Jake and Becky.

❄ ❄ ❄ ❄ ❄ ❄ ❄ ❄ ❄ ❄

In less than an hour Maggie learned the Thomas family tree—its members' honors, riches, and accomplishments. It was clear that Marie didn't picture herself on any particular branch. The girl had nearly opened up several times, but always backed off. At first Maggie didn't care if she ever found out what was making the girl so moody. Talk was talk and there wasn't much else to do. But as they spoke she found herself liking Marie more and more. Rich girl, yes. But not spoiled or dependent on her parents' money or even tied to their way of thinking. Whatever was on her mind didn't revolve around new cars or coats or whatever.

Maggie started to get up. Marie reached over and put her own hand lightly on Maggie's. "What you said a while ago—about strangers talking. If you had a really big problem, something that's nobody else's business . . . " Marie paused and Maggie realized that the girl could be talking about either of them. ". . . do you think strangers would listen? And could they keep a secret?"

"Honey, this stranger can keep any secret."

"Okay." Marie took a deep breath. "I'm pregnant." She immediately started crying. Maggie turned the girl away from the rest of her guests.

"I should have known." Maggie was feeling stupid. She should've known. How could she have missed it? "Now calm down. If you got a secret, let's not go telling everybody here."

"Does the father know?"

"He's long gone. It was a weekend thing."

"I know about that." Maggie shook her head. "I take it your parents don't know."

Marie shook her head. "They'd kill me."

"I doubt that, but I understand." Maggie understood all right. But she wondered whether to tell Marie. She had never shared her secret with anyone. Not in almost twenty years. It was one secret she had sworn never to share. Neither woman spoke. Maggie moved closer. Their heads nearly touched and for a moment Maggie's own brittle, salt-and-pepper hair seemed to mirror Marie's. Maggie moved close enough to feel Marie's breath.

Maggie inhaled, then in short little puffs exhaled. "There are things . . ." Maggie paused, collecting her thoughts. ". . . which I've never told another living soul. Things I'd just as soon never tell. But I'm gonna tell you." Marie started to draw back. Maggie raised one finger and Marie froze. "I'm gonna tell you because the problem you got, I've had. I may have been a little older—quite a bit older—but it was a problem all the same. And I had the same choices you got."

For only the second time since she'd walked into Holly Day's, Marie smiled. Her eyes watered slightly and the corners of her mouth turned up. She spoke in a whisper even though no one else would have heard.

"What did you do?"

"I thought about it long and hard. My mom and dad were already dead, so I couldn't tell 'em—not directly anyway. But I spoke to 'em in my thoughts and in the end I decided to have my baby."

"You did?" Marie's voice was hushed.

"I did and I gave it up. And the day has not gone by that it didn't pain me sorely." Maggie's own eyes watered. She turned away and wiped them with her sleeve. "But not once have I regretted my decision."

"And . . . and the baby?"

"Hon, I've told you more than I've ever told anyone. The rest goes with me to the grave."

"I didn't mean to pry."

"You didn't pry. All you did was listen. I'm the one prying. I just wanted you to know you're not alone. You got choices. Come to think of it, you've probably got one I didn't, and that's to keep him."

Marie reached out and grabbed Maggie's hand. "I'll keep your secret." Her eyes teared and she rolled them, embarrassed at the moment.

"Secrets are an awful load to bear," Maggie said. "I'm glad to have that one off my chest."

Maggie started to get up. Marie squeezed her hand tighter. "Thanks. I'll let you know."

"That's up to you, hon. But if you do let me know, I'll listen." Maggie stood up, took a deep breath, caught Will's eye, and gave the tip of her nose a squeeze.

CHAPTER 10

Pilgrims Together

LEO STROLLED UP TO THE OLD UPRIGHT like he was the evening's entertainment. Without a word of explanation he rolled back the thick canvas cover Maggie had draped over it years before. He sat down on the stool and pushed his index finger down on middle C.

A stunned silence followed. They were resigned to hardship. They were resigned to cold. They were resigned to the sparse food and spare comforts of Holly Day's. They weren't ready for Leo's decision to unearth the old piano. They weren't ready for the strident sound of his single off-key statement. Wood stoves were one thing—pianos another. Leo tried to tap out "Jingle Bells" . . . missed a note; tried again . . . missed another note.

Maggie watched from the shadows, alternately wincing and biting her lip. She hated to let him die up there by himself—even if he still deserved it for stealing her thunder. But what could she do? She hadn't played the piano for almost ten years. She hadn't played it in front of people for more than twenty. She'd almost surely make a fool of herself—though no worse than Leo. Cooking their food was one thing. Giving them the eight o'clock curtain was another.

Just when she had resolved to stay out of it, Leo hit three sour notes in a row. That decided the question. If she was going to jump in, she might as well do it head first and all at once. She strolled to the piano, calling out to Leo as she went.

"Hey, bub, it ain't no Steinway . . . but it ain't a set of drums either!"

"You can do better?" he countered with a big grin.

"Move over and watch a pro!"

Leo did as he was told and Maggie gave the piano stool a turn, as if that action was part of her act—and it was. Maggie hadn't forgotten. She'd done it too many times for too many years to forget. She jumped on and spun around to the keyboard. "Okay, let's start out light. I wanta hear 'Jingle Bells' sung real loud now."

Maggie's fingers came down on the keys and she started singing. "Jingle bells, jingle bells, jingle all the way . . ."

No one sang. They were cold and tired. It was hard enough just keeping the stove fired and getting the food cooked. Besides, they hadn't sung by themselves, let alone as part of a group, in years— some never. People just didn't do that anymore. Maggie could read their thoughts: "Just leave us alone, lady."

Julie started to sing but her words died when she realized no one else had joined her. Jake and Becky looked down, then away. They hadn't sung since their grandparents had hosted Christmas years before. Lanny continued staring out the window. His mind was locked on only one thing. Sarah wanted to help. She felt as embarrassed for Maggie as Maggie had for Leo, but that wasn't going to get her up on her feet, joining her daughter.

Then from his self-appointed post by the wood pile Zech Young stood up. ". . . oh what fun it is to ride in a one-horse open sleigh, hey!" He looked around with mock disgust. "If Miss Day can sing, we can sing. Come on! Jingle bells, jingle bells . . . "

Suddenly Becky and Jake joined in, then Sarah and Julie, and finally Lanny Hargrave. Liz sat for a moment in stunned silence. Was this the man who had ranted and raved all day? The aged TV huckster who could only focus with one-track ferocity on his errant children?

"Zech?" His name, as a question, popped out involuntarily.

"I like the holidays!" he roared. "The holidays were always good to Zech's!" He smiled and winked at Liz. She shrugged and joined in the singing.

The off-key piano and the discordant voices soon shook the walls. They were terrible, but loud. There was nothing else to do but join together and do their best. The harder they sang, the warmer they got and the closer they drew to each other. The Masters' baby woke up and didn't even cry. Instead it gurgled and cooed, reacting to the voices. They seemed drawn to the piano and before ten minutes had passed, they were leaning on and over it.

At one point Jake Masters lifted Julie up on top of the upright and she sat there like a miniature Lauren Bacall.

Leo, who had led, now followed. Even as he joined their singing, he watched Maggie do what she had once done better than anyone else on U.S. 31W—entertain her customers. Maybe she hadn't sung for a crowd in over twenty years, but it came back quickly. Even the voice wasn't too bad—a little raspy, but not too bad. Her vigor obscured the edge in her voice and eventually the edge itself passed. As her voice mellowed, so did Maggie.

One song followed another, then another. Some, like "Jingle Bells," they knew by heart. Others, like "White Christmas," they thought they knew, but didn't. That's when Maggie picked up the slack and stole the show. When they sang different words or started the wrong verse, they laughed at their mistakes and pushed on. But they kept trying and they kept calling out the names of songs.

❄ ❄ ❄ ❄ ❄ ❄ ❄ ❄ ❄ ❄

Will approached Marie Thomas like he would a movie star. He had failed once, he didn't want to fail again. He knew she was different. Her dress, her hair, the way she wore her makeup, her mannerisms, her rejection of even the simplest courtesy—all separated her from everyone else at Holly Day's. He caught her hiding in the shadows beyond the firelight, listening but not singing, clutching her fur tightly to her chest.

"You wouldn't be so cold if you tried singing." Will began to blush. He listened to his own voice and it sounded stupid.

"I'm not a singer."

"Neither are they . . . except for Maggie."

"Maggie's something." The softness in Marie's voice told Will all he needed to know.

"She's the best. She doesn't know it, but she is!"

For a minute or two they listened as Zech, then the rest, joined Maggie. Will didn't know what to say, but this time Marie seemed happy just to have his company. They sneaked glances at each other and squirmed in their chairs and listened, all the time wondering what they could talk about. When the first two songs ended, Maggie started polling the gathering for favorites. Will turned to Marie.

"I'll bet Christmas is a big deal with your family." He didn't know why he said it. Probably because he knew they had money, and money meant lots of presents.

Marie answered his statement with laughter colder than the

storm outside. At first he felt embarrassed, then angry at himself for saying whatever was so stupid, and finally angry at her for making him feel that way. She caught his hand and his emotions stopped.

"I'm sorry. Really. I wasn't laughing at you," she said. Will was as solid as his boss. She could see that right away. She also knew she had hurt his feelings. "When I was little we used to celebrate Christmas big time. Presents. A tree in every room. Big parties."

"Church caroling?" That was something Will had always done with Oma and Jasper.

"Uh . . . no," Marie sighed. "Then as I got older, it seemed like everyone just got busy at Christmas. Presents still, but a lot of travel—Dad to Colorado, Mom to New York. My older brother went skiing with guys from college. I used to get really down."

"That's too bad." His eyes lit up. "Maybe you could celebrate with Maggie and me . . . at least until it stops snowing and you can get back on the road."

She looked straight into his eyes and realized he wasn't using a line on her, trying to get something from her. He wasn't like the guys at school. He wasn't like the guy she'd only seen for a weekend.

"You really mean it, don't you?"

"Of course I mean it. I can see why you're looking so sad. I would too if I couldn't feel good about going home for Christmas." She didn't respond. For an instant it looked as if she could either cry or hit him. Will didn't reach out, but he didn't retreat. He was there to listen—just as he always had for Maggie.

Without any more said, Marie started rambling and didn't stop. She talked about her times as a little girl at Christmas. She told Will about friends from childhood whom she hoped to see when she got home. She talked about her parents and how much they'd grown apart. She talked about school, her roommate, the course she was sure she failed, the exam she hadn't studied for, the paper she would have aced if she hadn't waited to start it until the night before it was due. Then she stopped, took a deep breath, and while the other guests were singing at the top of their lungs, leaned over and said very precisely.

"I've done something really stupid." Her hands dropped to her side. Her coat slipped open. Will looked, but couldn't see a thing in the dark.

"Well, I don't know what you did, but that's no reason to be miserable on Christmas Eve."

"Isn't it? You don't know my father—," she thought for a second, "or my mother."

"It can't be that bad! No matter what, it's Christmas!" He spoke the word "Christmas" as if its mention alone would mean something to her.

"Look, I'll bet your parents don't expect you to be perfect. Mine do!"

Will diverted his eyes. He could feel his ears flaming red. Neither he nor Marie spoke for several seconds. When he spoke it was in quick, embarrassed spurts.

"I guess not. I mean, I guess my parents aren't worried about that! I don't think so anyway. I mean, I don't have any parents. At least I don't have any who claim me. I had a mother all right, but she gave me away. At least my Aunt Oma and Uncle Jasper took me in. Not that they needed another kid. But they did anyway. They're good people—but they're not parents . . ."

"Your parents gave you away?" Marie was incredulous. She lived in a world of adoptions, not foundlings.

"Yeah, I was a kind of Christmas present. Left me right inside the church." Will laughed nervously, tugging at his reddened ear. "There was a service going on. It wasn't like she left me to die in the cold or anything."

"That's hideous."

"I don't know . . . she must have known she couldn't take care of me. Lots of other folks have. I've been pretty lucky."

"Lucky! You've got to be kidding!"

"Nah . . . she probably didn't have much money. It's a cinch she wasn't married to my father. I've wondered sometimes if he ever knew. But anyway, things turned out okay."

"Have you ever wished you weren't born?" Her voice was hollow, addressing an empty space in her own soul.

Will took her question seriously, pondering the possibility, turning it all over in his mind. "No . . . no, I haven't. Can't say I've ever thought about it. I mean I've thought about my real parents, but not about not being born. I guess I could've, but really I've had it pretty good. Uncle Jasper's a little rough, but Aunt Oma's a pretty good lady. Then there's Maggie—I've known her as long as I can remember."

"You know what my problem is, don't you?" She spoke without affection.

Will flushed again, embarrassed not by his knowledge but by his lack of it.

"Well, uh, not really."

"You know what your mother's problem was . . ."

"Yeah . . ."

"Well . . ." Marie had opened up. Now he was registering nothing but a slight look of amazement. ". . . you're making this awfully hard on me!"

Will didn't know what to say. For some reason he just didn't think rich girls got in trouble. But he was afraid to say that.

"I'm sorry," he finally stuttered. "I just didn't think . . . well, what I mean is . . . well, does your boyfriend know?"

"Boyfriend!" she laughed, throwing back her head. "He wasn't exactly a boyfriend. I was sort of the fraternity mascot. On our one weekend he called me the 'sweet tart of Sigma Chi.'"

"Sounds like a nice guy." Will arched his brows, stood up, and started shuffling from one foot to another.

"He was good looking and had money."

"There you go," Will nodded matter-of-factly, "they're always the biggest creeps."

Marie laughed, this time with genuine pleasure at Will's simple pronouncement. "I think you're right. I wish I'd known it back then."

"Does he know?"

"I don't want him to know." Her manic laughter subsided. "I don't want anyone to know."

"You sound pretty down."

"Yeah, I guess I am," she said. "Maybe I wish I hadn't been so lucky when the cars all skidded off the highway."

"I wouldn't wish that."

"I wouldn't know the difference if it killed me quickly."

"Maybe not, but you might end up paralyzed or something. Besides, it would be hell on your parents."

"They wouldn't care. Sometimes I wish I could just do it myself."

"A friend of mine from high school did the number with his girlfriend. Hooked up the exhaust pipe with a garden hose and they both fell asleep. They found them the next morning. It didn't solve a damned thing."

Marie paled. She looked like she might throw up. Will made a motion toward her and she took a deep breath.

"I'm okay. I'm okay,"

"You don't look okay."

"No, I'm fine. Really." She glanced up. There were finally tears in her eyes. "You know, I wish I'd known someone like you at Vandy."

"Hold on 'till next year and I might see you there." Will smiled as if he knew a secret. "'Course, you might not want to talk to me with all of your other friends around."

She started to respond but couldn't. Then she took a deep breath.

"Would *you* talk to me? That's the question."

"What? Are you serious? I mean, sure. Of course I'd talk to you! I mean, we're practically spending Christmas together!" Will's words tumbled about as he fumbled to say the right thing.

Marie saved him. "Tell me more now. Tell me why you love Maggie so much. Tell me what she'll do when we all leave."

While the others sang, Will started talking. He answered her questions and she answered his. Moments before she had been an island by herself. He had been more of an adult than a boy, helping out, making things work. They had handled the weighty topics, nothing resolved but nothing unresolvable. Now they were both eighteen again, no more, no less. Time was forever. The world around them had been placed there for their education. Movies and music, classes and course work. Life unfolding. They found common ground, probing around with their questions until they connected. They talked a mile a minute until the subject was exhausted. Then they started another. All for fun, just spending time. Blanketed in the warmth of the fire, with the singing voices as background, they eased into knowing each other.

❋　❋　❋　❋　❋　❋　❋　❋　❋　❋

After each song Maggie glanced over at Will and Marie, leaning toward each other as they spoke, smiling more as the moments gathered into an hour. Something good was happening over there. Marie of the Chicago Thomases wasn't so bad after all. First impressions weren't always right. Her eyes scanned the room.

Julie was fading, nodding more and more during the past few carols. Sarah seemed content for the first time that day, her arm around Julie's shoulders as she nodded off. Zech had sung louder than anyone else and even soloed on a Hanukkah song—though he had been urged to the performance by Maggie. He insisted he was perfectly happy celebrating Irving Berlin's success in writing "White Christmas." Becky tended her baby, but constantly nudged Jake into singing with the others. Lanny seemed to watch out the window just a little bit less and pay just a little bit more attention to the world inside Holly Day's. Leo mostly stood to the side and grinned.

When Maggie started singing "I'll Be Home For Christmas," the others started to fumble along. They meant well and they didn't want her to feel all alone. For more than an hour that's what they had been doing and they didn't want to stop now. But as Maggie's voice rose above the others, something happened. Jake and Becky didn't know the words; Julie was fast asleep; Sarah didn't remember more than the first few lines; Zech and Liz knew the words but were happier just letting Maggie take the center stage; Will and Marie ceased their nonstop banter and sat quietly, in awe. Leo nodded his head like a satisfied teacher. They were her guests as well as her customers. More importantly, they were an audience.

The moment was Maggie's, her fingers making the old piano sound as if it was tuned. She recalled Christmases past in the glisten of her eye and the lilt in her voice. But even as she evoked the past, it was Maggie's opportunity to live again in the present. Her test to pass or fail. She sang and they listened. She stared into the glow of the wood stove and beyond into the endless stretches of wherever home was for Christmas. And as she sang, she realized that wherever home was for the others, she was already there. The past, the present, and the future all merged. Home for Christmas. It wasn't a place on earth, it was a place in the heart. And she was finally there again.

The song ended. She looked around. Everyone's eyes, except Julie's which were closed, were on her. They applauded. Zech nodded and murmured, "*Shalom.*" They spoke soft thanks, acknowledging the community that even now made them uncomfortable.

"Thanks, folks," Maggie said. Her voice was husky and she cleared her throat.

Suddenly Leo was by her side again. She started to get up and he put his arm around her. "You did yourself proud," he said. She looked at him and blushed.

"My pleasure," she said.

The room was silent, almost reverent for the moment that was passing. For an instant it looked like they would all disperse to their blanket-filled chairs encircling the stove. Then Leo started talking.

"During all the years my kids were little, I never did get home for Christmas Eve. My wife did all the work at home. Most of the time I got home Christmas Day. Don't know why, it just worked out that way. But we always talked. I'd catch her right about now—'bout eleven. And I'd tell her where I was and what I'd been doing. And we'd talk and tell funny stories." He paused, looking around the room. "Sarah, I'll bet you got a tale or two you could share. You too, Zech. And Maggie, I *know* you've got some stories to tell!"

Sarah started to shake her head, then looked at Leo and knew he wouldn't let her off. "Okay," she began, "one Christmas Eve I got up way too early . . . I was about six. I came downstairs and I can still remember how quickly my father scooted me up in his arms. 'Santa's in the next room,' he whispered. 'We can't say a word or he'll get away before he's left all of the presents.' And my father took me up to my little twin bed—my sister was fast asleep right next to me—tucked me in, and started whispering, 'Twas the night before Christmas, and all through the house . . .' I only remember him saying the first couple of lines, then I must have fallen asleep."

"Your father still around?" Leo asked.

Sarah hesitated. "Yes, he is. But he lives in . . . well, he and my mother divorced when I was a teenager. I don't see him and his new wife much."

"Drop in on him," Leo said. "I'll bet he's expecting you."

"Oh no . . ." she started.

"Oh yes." Leo smiled. "It'll be okay."

Sarah drew a breath. There was such a sense of certainty about him. Not overbearing or strong-armed, but firm and precise. She nodded and found herself saying okay. Maybe that thought had been with her all along. She didn't think so, but maybe it had. In any event, she felt as if she had just made a promise.

Leo turned to Maggie. "And your tales?"

She smiled. "After you."

Leo grinned and didn't argue. He told of cross-country trips in snow four feet deep. He talked about having to deliver a shipment of Cabbage Patch dolls from Chicago to San Francisco, crossing the Rockies in an ice storm. "I really felt like Santa Claus that night," he laughed. "It was about a week before Christmas—and I was carrying all of the back orders!" He recalled one really good Christmas, driving his rig up into his front yard and parking it there just after midnight. The family hadn't gone to sleep. He was their best Christmas gift that year. He didn't stop to get teary eyed, but rolled on from one story to another. They were as many and as different as the roads he drove.

Maggie started with stories from the early fifties. "I was barely a child," she lied with a click of her tongue on the roof of her mouth. "Things were pretty hot over in Korea back then. Those army boys were desperate to get assigned or go home!" She sighed. "But we made sure they were well fed and had some hot coffee before we let 'em get back on the road. We were the unofficial USO in these parts!

"One Christmas," she continued, "we had a bunch of little kids stopping with their parents on the way to Grandma's and Grandpa's. Must have been '54, maybe '55. Anyway, they really needed something to cheer 'em up before they crawled into the back seat of their old Nash and headed on. It was like having a room full of little Julies!"

At the mention of her name Julie sat up, then slumped back down and fell asleep against Sarah's shoulder.

"We read 'em Christmas stories," Maggie continued. "Collected up all of the books we could find and read 'em one by one. Then we sang 'Rudolph the Red-Nosed Reindeer'—that was still real popular back then. Mom and Dad were better than Gene Autry. They were beautiful together."

"What about Holly?" Sarah asked. She had wondered about the café's namesake since the afternoon.

"Yeah," Leo's voice gently chided from the shadows, "what about Holly?"

"Holly sang the best of all." Maggie let Leo know by her look that the subject was closed.

"That so?" Leo said.

Zech interjected, "You know, Christmas is a lot of things to a lot of people. Birth of Jesus, winter solstice, yule log celebration, Hanukkah, or whatever. And it was always the best time for retail sales!"

"Zech's was the best store in Bowling Green," Maggie interjected. "I did all of my Christmas shopping there."

Zech beamed with pleasure. "That's what I was getting at. You know it was a great month for sales, but December was a great time for feeling good too. People came in. Not just Bowling Green but all of the stores. I traveled to every one of them. And I saw their faces. People who really wanted to find something special for someone else. That's how it used to be at least."

Lanny Hargrave seemed to awaken from his dazed vigil and wandered over toward the fire. "I remember Zech's," he said simply. "I got my boy's high school class ring at Zech's. Got my wife our tenth anniversary present there too!" Lanny smiled for the first time that day.

"And was she happy with it?" Zech was eager for his answer, still thriving on customers' good reviews.

"She loved it, Zech. Matter of fact, I've been meaning to tell you how my boy and I used to watch your late night show on Friday."

"Yeah," Maggie chimed in, "I remember Zech's All Night Theatre. You introduced 'em and gave a little story about every movie."

"I selected all the movies myself! They tried to sell me packages, but I got what I wanted."

"No!" Maggie leaned against the piano. "I always thought those movies were the best on TV before cable . . ."

"And they were! But I had to fight the damned stations. They wanted all Japanese monster movies! I insisted on good stuff. Gary Cooper and Barbara Stanwyck and Spencer Tracy and Katherine Hepburn and Bette Davis and Henry Fonda—only the best! You'd be surprised what they'll cram down your throat if you don't watch out. They always figure color is better than black and white."

"You had my business up in Louisville," Sarah nestled Julie more carefully onto her lap, "if you count a ten-year-old's Christmas present for her fifth-grade crush!"

"The younger the better at Zech Young's!" Zech clapped his hands together, seeming to dismiss ten years from his age at the bat of an eye. "What were the ten-year-olds buying that year, my dear?"

Sarah blushed, wishing she hadn't offered recollections of Christmas past. Personal details of any sort were just that. She revealed her past as if she were doling out treasured and long-hidden sweets.

"I'll bet I can guess," Zech persisted. "Was it an identification bracelet? Or maybe a silver football on a chain? No . . . I know . . ." Zech paused and Sarah's usually strained expression melted into the face of a little girl. ". . . I'll bet you bought him a Mispah. Right?"

Julie looked up, more awake than she had been letting on. "What's a Miz . . ."

"Mispah, darling. It's a broken heart, or really two halves which together make a whole heart. It was sterling silver and some boy got one half and your mother the other," her mother answered. Sarah turned to the old man. "You're right, Zech. The Mispah broken heart . . . that was it when I was ten! And not too smart about broken hearts since then!"

"Honey," Maggie slapped her thighs, "if I had a dime every time my heart broke, I'd be one rich lady."

Sarah looked away. "I'm not proud of my broken hearts."

"If we didn't have hearts to break, we wouldn't be human," Maggie said.

"And it's not always men who break hearts," Liz interjected. "Sometimes its children . . . right, Zech?"

"They took what I had and turned it to junk! I probably should have sold it outright, or stuck with it through the eighties. Wal-Mart—yes—but we could have survived. I had some ideas, but the kids—my son and daughter—they couldn't agree on the ad for the Sunday paper!"

"Don't blame yourself," Maggie sighed. "I couldn't get fifty bucks for this place." She realized what she had said and looked around for Will. He was still out of hearing range, talking with Marie.

"But let's get back to stories." Zech was sorry they had spun off into the jewelry store's misfortunes. "I loved being in the shop back then. When the men would come in to buy something special for their wives for Christmas they always put on a mumble and grumble about having to shop. I'd go along with them for a while, but before too long I'd show them something and their eyes would light up and I could see that little spark . . . that spirit people talk about at this time of year." Zech hesitated for an instant. "I wonder if my children ever saw that spark."

"At least you all had jobs for most of your lives." Jake Masters had been helping Becky change the baby, but with crumpled diaper in hand, and at least laughing, he entered the conversation. "I dropped out of high school thinkin' I'd have it like my dad! Boy, talk about dumb!"

"You're going to do okay, son." Leo came over to Jake and rested his meaty hand on the boy's shoulder.

"Not with my luck."

"You never know. Luck changes. It really does. A spot might open up somewhere."

"I missed the interview today!"

"Well, let me tell you," Leo reached into his pocket and withdrew a soft, well-worn business card, "here's the group I've been working with and I wouldn't be surprised if they had an opening somewhere along the line."

"Do you think so?" Jake's voice immediately picked up.

"I'd be willing to bet on it . . . but I'll tell you now, make that young lady and that little guy number-one priority. Make time for them first. It's short. Trust me, life's short."

Jake nodded emphatically. "I think you're right, Leo. In fact, I know you're right."

And so the talk went. One hour sliding into another. One story melding with the many before it. Sarah drifted off, then Becky, then Jake. Lanny went back to his place at the front window and Zech and Liz dozed in each other's arms. Will left Marie when her eyes became too heavy to keep open and he joined Leo and Maggie who remained near the front counter. It was when the three of them were seated in a circle, the fire recently stoked by Will's ready supply of wood, that Leo turned to Maggie and smiled.

"Now, Holly, tell me all about yourself."

CHAPTER 11

Toward Midnight

AT FIRST MAGGIE WAS SILENT. Will didn't move. He wasn't certain what Leo had said. If he had called her Holly, he wasn't sure why. Either the old trucker was losing it, or he was on the verge of insight. Leo leaned forward, oblivious to Will's incredulous looks, and stared unblinkingly at the older woman.

"My name's Maggie," she broke the silence. "It's always been Maggie. It's always going to be Maggie."

"Right you are."

"Then why do you keep calling me names you got no business calling me!"

Leo's smile was beguiling, filled with humor but at the same time understanding, absent of malice or condescension. It reached out to Maggie and told her that all of the lonely years had, after all, been well spent. "You're an actress, Holly *Margaret* Day. You play your part well, but you can't fool old Leo. You're Holly to me, and you'll always be Holly to me."

He turned to Will. "You can trust me on that!"

"Maggie?" Will began, "Holly . . . ?"

"Don't pay any attention to him, Will. The fellow's been drinking. Maybe the blizzard's got his brain."

"Believe me, Will," Leo continued, "I'm not telling stories now!"

"You think you can call me Holly—just like that—take my dead sister's name and use it for your crazy ideas. Well, I got news for you, you don't know me at all!"

"Sure I do."

"How's that? Where from? Tell me that, Mr. Wise Guy. When did you know me or Holly?"

"A long time ago . . . seems like forever."

"You're not old enough."

"I've been around. You can trust me on that too."

Maggie fixed her hardest stare on him. Seconds passed. Then she spoke, slowly and precisely.

"Nobody's left in Christian who remembers Holly Day. That was thirty-some years ago or more. People who remembered Holly are dead or moved away." Her stare intensified. "And I still say you're not old enough to remember Holly."

Leo leaned back, staring outside at the snow. The storm had let up, the clouds had begun to blow out to the east, and moonlight was causing the snowdrifts to glisten like ice cream cones. "You'd be surprised. Memories are long on the road. They get shared and they become a part of you."

"Look, Leo, you're tired. It's been a long day. Maybe you been drinking. That's okay. I could use a drink right now myself."

"For old time's sake?"

"Now look, there are no old times. Before tonight I'd never met you!"

"Sure we met . . . plenty of times."

"You're nuts!"

"One Christmas you served me hot chocolate and told me a story about how your parents broke into vaudeville. I was just a kid—no older than Jake Masters over there."

Maggie blinked twice. Remembrances registered and she tried to square them with the bearded man seated by her in the light of the fire. "I remember that. I do. But I don't remember you!"

"You stroked my head and told me I counted for something."

"That was a teary eyed kid. You . . . I mean the kid had just broke up with his girl. But that was . . ."

"A long time ago. Yeah, you're right. Another time you gave me a free meal when I didn't have a buck on me."

"No . . . no . . . that wasn't the same guy. I would have remembered."

"Then one Christmas Eve you paid my family's bus fare to come see me when I was down and out."

"That was almost forty years ago. I know. Now stop it!"

"Years go by like days sometimes. Times get all jumbled."

"Not that jumbled," Maggie insisted. The color was rising in her face. "It couldn't have been you. Not any of those times. You may have heard stories. Sure, lots of stories get passed up and down this old stretch of 31W. But it wasn't you! That last guy you described was a black guy. Hah!" She turned to Will and winked. The boy's mouth was open in dumb wonder at the things he was hearing.

"You're right . . . but I still remember. Now tell Will that you're not Holly."

Maggie's bravado melted. She turned to Will and sighed. It was confession time. She couldn't fight the man any longer. She didn't even want to. It had been so awfully long since anyone had called her Holly and it felt so good. "The old boy's got me there, Will. I'm guilty as charged. No use denying it anymore."

Will sprang up as if hit with a cattle prod, then slowly slipped back down in his chair and gulped. "You're Holly?"

Maggie became girlish, looking down and away. "That's what I said."

"But why?" Will exclaimed. "Why the big story? Why did it make any difference?"

"Things always make a difference. Big difference, little difference." She paused, not quite ready for an answer to Will's question.

Leo interceded. "Holly died when the café started dying, Will. Right?"

Maggie nodded. "Pop died. Then Mom. I fell in love with some guy that got assigned to guarding the line in Korea. He got himself killed. Then the interstate came through and changed everything. Holly Day's turned into a dinosaur and Christian got real quiet."

"Holly Day was the queen of a real joint, Will," Leo added, "a first-class, 'round-the-clock, hopping juke joint. The café was famous, Will. Holly was to these parts what little old Rosie Clooney was to Maysville up on the river. But the café ended and there wasn't much left for Holly. Right?"

"Right," she said. "End of café—end of Holly. Everything was changing, but I didn't want it to. I wanted something to remain. So I decided to save my memories. If I had to go on, fine. But Mom and Dad and Holly would all be a lot safer in my memories."

"So you created your sainted sister and she lived on in your stories." Leo rubbed his palms together as he helped Maggie fill in the blanks for Will. "But tell me this, Miss Holly Margaret Day, didn't it feel like Holly again today? Didn't it feel like she was back alive again?"

Maggie considered his question, staring at his hands as she extended her own toward the fire. She looked into Leo's eyes. "It did indeed, Mr. DeAngelis. It did indeed." She spoke more softly than Will had ever heard.

Will leaned back and shook his head. "I never thought adults could act so crazy!"

"Life's gonna have some surprises for you, Will Joseph," Maggie chided him. "That *is* for sure."

With her own secret revealed, Maggie's thoughts raced back to the truck driver who claimed to be so many of her past Christmas visitors. "But Leo . . . what about those times you said I helped you years ago?"

Leo smiled and prepared to answer, then stopped. The big man seemed to lose his breath for an instant, then he inhaled, reacting in surprise as if something or someone had just touched him from behind in a darkened room. He looked outside. The snow had stopped completely. The moon was almost full and the countryside was one vast panorama of reflected moonlight.

"Storm's lifted. I gotta get goin'." He stood up and quickly buttoned his thick plaid coat. Then he smiled. "Gotta get that fruit to the grocers. It's probably froze up as it is!"

"Just like that?" Maggie protested. "I call your bluff and you're ready to bolt! You're just touchy about having to 'fess up to your own tall tales!"

Leo grinned. "All your customers have had to move on sooner or later, Holly my dear. Now it's *my* time."

"I wanta know what other secrets you got on Maggie!" Will joked. "Where are all the other skeletons?"

Leo looked at Will, then Maggie, and winked at her. "Always keep the boy guessing," he said.

"I wish you'd stay 'til dawn," Maggie urged. "It's liable to be rough out there still. You don't know if the road's open or not."

"I think my road's wide open now. I might even make it home for Christmas after all." Leo reached inside of his coat pocket and removed an old silver dollar. He held it toward Maggie. "This has been my lucky piece for a long time. When Julie wakes up, tell her Santa Claus came while we were all asleep and left it for her. Tell the others that I enjoyed their company." He paused to collect his words. "Will, I'm gonna miss your help. But I'll be checking on you. Knowing how good you are in school, I'll bet you end up a doctor . . . or even a preacher. You got a lotta good in you. You need to let it come out somehow." He turned to Maggie. "Keep him safe, Holly. He's a damned lucky boy to have as . . . well, he's a real lucky boy. You remember that too, Will Joseph."

"I will. You bet."

"I hope I didn't step on your toes too much, Holly." The big man reached over and gave his hostess a hug, followed by a kiss on the cheek. It sent a shiver through her. "I'll miss you more than you'll know. You keep plugging away. You're gonna be okay. Trust me on that too!"

Leo gazed around at the cafe one last time. "You know, Holly, Will might be right about this old place. You could move it closer to the interstate. A joint like this just might take off. Kinda catchy and old fashioned. And old Zech Young could be the guy to give you some help. What do you think, Will?"

"Well, that's a great idea . . . I mean, that's what I've been trying to convince her of all along."

Leo nodded and drew the door toward him. A gust of wind blew in.

"Wait." Maggie stopped him. He let the door ease shut again. "Just tell me one thing . . . just one . . . why didn't you just let me stay Maggie?"

"Maggie was a good old gal," Leo smiled. "Full of piss and vinegar and a lot of fight—but so's Holly—and she's got a heart that's not afraid to soar a little. Maggie started hiding her heart a long time ago. You'll be needing that heart no matter what you do from here on."

Maggie grabbed his sleeve. "What about your Christmas present? You won the bet about starting the stove . . . I owe you something."

"I've gotten my present—you gave it to me tonight, over on the piano and right now. That's all I need."

Maggie started to argue with him, to use some device to make him stay a while longer, but she could see that he was leaving this time. "Come by again," she urged. "I mean it. Anytime."

Leo opened the door again and looked back at them. "I'll be looking out for you two," he grinned. "I'll send you all the pilgrims you can serve. Rain or snow or fair weather. Take care now, and Merry Christmas." Then he turned and was gone. For a moment all of the life seemed to leave Holly Day's Café. Then Maggie turned to Will and as he caught her up in a hug, it quickly returned.

CHAPTER 12

The Last Pilgrim Arrives

BUDDY WENDELL'S LIGHTS PLAYED OFF THE SNOW like leap-frogging ghosts. It had been ten minutes since Leo had exited Holly Day's, yet Maggie and Will hadn't said a word. They sat immersed in their own thoughts, comforted by each other's presence, but not compelled to pour out their feelings. Will didn't ask any of the questions racing through his mind and Maggie didn't offer any further explanations for Holly's life and death. Time for those words could wait. It had been quite a day—and quite a night—and now it was the dark hours of Christmas morning.

They were both spent, too tired to move when Buddy's state-owned four-wheel drive careened around the corner of Main Street and headed straight for the café. Buddy had been gone for more than twelve hours—it seemed more like days. Anything could have happened in that time. Buddy had been out all day. He could be half frozen. He could have been in an accident. Yet Maggie was slow to stand up, and Will slower still, as the outline of Buddy's vehicle appeared in the moonlight.

But if Maggie and Will seemed half dead, Lanny Hargrave was suddenly electric with life. The old man had been napping too near the window to stay warm. The wood stove's radiance faded that far away, yet Lanny was right where he wanted to be for his lookout. He had wrapped his blanket tightly around himself to stay

103

warm and as he sprung awake he looked like some poor soul sewn up in a straightjacket. It was Lanny struggling with his covers that energized Maggie. Will simply followed.

"Lanny," she said, turning toward him, "it's Buddy. It's just Buddy." She moved to him as she spoke. Lanny had unloosened himself and was pressed against the frosted front window of the café.

Lanny faced Maggie as she reached his side. "It's Frank," he said. His voice was thick and uneven. "Frank's come back."

"No, Lanny," Maggie took his arm, "it's Buddy. Buddy Wendell."

But no sooner had she spoken than Buddy planted his four-wheeler at the café's front door, rushed to the passenger side, and opened it to reveal a passenger slumped backwards in the front seat. Will had moved to the front door and opened it as Buddy turned toward him.

"Give me a hand, Will. This boy's a mite heavy."

Will started forward, but before he could get two feet out the front door Lanny had rushed past him and down the steps. Will stumbled over a snowdrift, then caught his balance and found Maggie standing next to him.

"Good Lord!" Maggie exclaimed. "This I don't believe." She watched as Lanny Hargrave caught the crumpled figure in his arms and single-handedly swept him onto the porch and into Holly Day's. Buddy struggled through the drifts, trying to keep up with Lanny.

Maggie grabbed him by the sleeve. "Buddy, where'd ya find him?"

"Who is he?" Will interrupted.

Maggie turned to Will, her eyes registering disbelief. "That, Will Joseph, is Frank Hargrave. Frank Hargrave come home at last."

"Good Lord!" Will mimicked his boss. "I was beginning to think he wasn't real."

"He was real all right," Maggie rejoined, "just not around here."

Lanny tended to his son as if he were a little boy who had stayed out too long sledding. He sat him in a chair near the fire, leaned him back, started fiddling with his coat, and generally tended him back to life.

"He's lucky to be alive," Buddy nodded toward Frank. "He must have pulled his car off the exit after his tire blowed or whatever. It was flat and froze hard as a rock. He was smart enough to stay in his car most of the day and night. He only had on a light trench coat. The snow must have caught him by surprise. He would have died for sure if he'd left that car. He almost died sitting out there as it was. We were working so hard on the highway we didn't see him and I guess he didn't see us either."

"Is he going to be okay?" Will asked.

"He's coming around. He pinked up a little once I got him in the four-by-four. He must've run out of gas around ten or so. He's been mostly out of it, but he's asked for Lanny and I knew he'd be here."

Buddy had just spoken when Frank's eyes opened and he found Lanny rubbing his hands and legs, getting his circulation going again. Frank looked up and blinked. "Dad?" His voice was hoarse, a raspy whisper, but Lanny heard him. He grabbed up his son and crushed him to his chest.

"Dad," the younger man stated more clearly. Then he repeated the word over and over again as Lanny held him up in his arms, alternately murmuring his son's name and thanking God.

Zech Young and Jake Masters had awakened. In a few minutes so had the others, except Julie. They didn't interrupt father and son. They didn't say a word. They just encircled them, patting Lanny on the back and letting him know they understood his joy.

"Pretty rough out there?" Will asked Buddy. The sight of father and son together made him want to cry, so he found other things to talk about.

"Should be clear by first light," Buddy said. "Guess people can go home for Christmas after all!" Buddy looked toward the stove and the collection of sleeping guests. "Hate for you to lose so many pay customers."

"Yeah," Maggie cocked her eye at him, "all the big spenders always hang out at Holly's!"

"Well, it's better than being alone on Christmas!"

Buddy's statement was simple enough, but it was the first time Maggie had thought of it that way. If it hadn't been for the storm she would have never had guests on Christmas Eve. She would have been alone—even Will would have returned to Oma and Jasper. She might have given into her thoughts about collecting the insurance on the café or even herself. And she would never have met Leo and the others, never have cooked for a crowd again, never have sung until her voice was gone.

"Right you are, Buddy. Right you are."

"So, everyone's safe and sound?"

"Yeah." Maggie nodded. "That little girl almost got killed when the tree knocked down a power line, but Leo caught her before she could get to it."

"So which one's Leo?" Buddy grinned. "I always like to meet a hero."

"Leo's left already," Will said.

"What was he driving, a dog sled?"

"Leo won't have any problem . . . he'll get his rig to Cincinnati before you know it!" Will was quick to brag on the big bearded man.

"You should have passed him on the way in . . . he was on foot," Maggie added.

"Nobody on foot out there . . . 'less they went through the woods I would've passed 'em."

"Well maybe he did take a short cut . . . he's a pretty clever guy," Maggie added.

"But you said he had a rig?"

"Yeah, big semi. Said he sort of started the problems on the highway . . . spinning his trailer or whatever."

"Well, there was a big rig on the highway, but that wasn't your boy."

"I'll bet it was," Will chided.

"I'll bet the ranch it wasn't," Buddy chided back. "This rig was in no shape to go anywhere . . . it was jackknifed and turned over."

Will glanced at Maggie and Maggie at Will. Leo had seemed so certain about going back to his rig. They could read each other's thoughts: Leo must have been confused. At the least he didn't remember that his truck was out of commission.

"Maybe we better go look for him, Buddy." Will was already buttoning his coat and opening the door.

"Well, maybe it's a different rig . . . cause this driver's not going anywhere either."

"What d'ya mean, Buddy?" Maggie started fidgeting with her sweater.

"Well, for starters, I heard on the radio that he just died."

"Just died?" Will wondered if he had heard Buddy right. He closed the door and came back to Buddy. "Who just died?"

"The trucker whose rig overturned. Poor guy hung on all day. Never did come around though. Matter of fact, when we got him back to Bowling Green the docs acted like he should have been dead already. But he had a helluva heart!"

"You saw this fellow?" Will asked his question in a sleepwalker's monotone.

"Caught a glimpse of him . . . my partner handled most of that."

"What did he look like, Buddy?" Maggie's voice was faint, far away.

"He was a good-sized boy . . . bushy old red beard." Buddy paused as Maggie dropped into the nearest chair. "Say, what's wrong? Don't tell me you knew him?" Buddy paused again, but Maggie didn't answer. "Old customer or something?"

"I knew a guy like that," Maggie's voice was barely a whisper, "but there's a lot of bearded truckers on the road."

"Sorry to say this guy won't be anymore. Say listen, do you suppose I could go over and get a fresh cup of coffee?"

"Go ahead," was all that Maggie could muster.

Once Buddy was out of hearing range Will drew his chair up closely to Maggie. Maggie was staring outside, unblinking, her mouth frozen in a tight smile.

"Maggie, I'm shivering all over . . . tell me I'm dreaming what Buddy just told us."

Maggie turned to Will, her smile softening through warm tears. She reached over and placed her hand on his cheek. For a moment she seemed to be collecting her thoughts. "Will, I don't think we were dreaming about anything. Not a thing."

"Do we tell the others?" Will was sputtering for explanations. He wanted to tell everyone, but he was afraid to tell anyone.

Maggie looked at the silver dollar entrusted to her care. She squeezed it tight, then tucked it carefully away for Julie. It was as real as Leo—flesh or spirit, man or ghost. She looked into Will's eyes.

"Buddy'll be gone soon. He won't tell 'em anything and neither will we. Then they'll leave . . . and they'll only know what their hearts and minds tell 'em. They'll remember us and Leo and Lanny and his son, and Holly Day's Café . . . and it'll be a Christmas they talk about the rest of their lives."

Will knelt down next to her chair and took her hand.

"Merry Christmas, Holly Day." He pronounced her name with dignity.

She giggled like a little girl. "Merry Christmas, son."

Molly's Santa Claus

Molly's Santa Claus

"SANTA CLAUS IS HERE! Dad! Tad! Mom! Come quick! Santa Claus is here!" Molly was standing outside at the front gate screaming loud enough for everyone in the neighborhood to hear. As a matter of fact, the Melrose sisters live three doors down and they told us two days later that they had heard her! They were pretty nice about it— for the old maid Melrose sisters anyway—even though they did slip in a dig about missing a full five minutes of "Wheel of Fortune." But anyway, Molly kept calling out in a voice ten times too big for her six years, "Come quick. Somebody. Come quick. Santa Claus is here. Quick!"

Molly had gone outside a second or two before to stare up at the stars and look at the lights Dad had just finished stringing over the doorway. Mom and Dad call her their junior astronomer. I call her the sophomore space cadet! She was supposed to be killing time while Mom finished getting ready and Dad was on the kitchen telephone rounding up his last victims for volunteer church service. Of course, Mom wasn't about to come downstairs without her makeup even if Molly had been yelling, "Murder! Police! Murder!" Mom has her standards.

Dad was standing with his right finger in his ear trying to blot Molly out. "Come on, Fred. It won't be more than an hour or two. We'll pop some corn, serve some punch, and be on our way." Poor

111

Dad. The man is the original defender of the lost cause. I was in the study trying to watch some TV and I could see Dad and Molly both. "Just a second, Fred. No . . . no . . . it will be just a second!" Dad pressed the mouthpiece into his chest.

"What is it, honey?"

Then Molly's voice again. "Come quick, it's Santa Claus!"

Then Dad, even louder: "What is it, honey?"

Then Molly, even screechier: "I can't hear you. Come quick!"

Now I could have let this opera of the deaf and dumb go on forever. After all, I was trying to concentrate. But Dad and Molly kept yelling back and forth, neither one of them budging from their God-given right to make the other one come to them.

Personally, I didn't care if we ever went down to the mission to serve snacks and stuff. Not that I minded. I'd done it once or twice before, but this was Dad's baby. On the other hand, I felt sorry for him. Fred Smitherfield was the fifth caller in ten minutes trying to back out of community service two days before Christmas.

It was time for someone to compromise! "I'll see what she wants!" I yelled. I thought this was pretty big of me. I heard a fainter "Thanks, Tad," from the kitchen, then the resumption of my dad's pleading with Smitherfield.

I sprang from the couch and headed out the side door. I was lucky I didn't kill myself, because Molly had left her bicycle at the foot of the porch steps, but in the starlight I saw the shine of the chrome and jigged to the right, then to the left. I was nearly to the front of the house and pretty darned mad by the time I caught my balance. I had forgotten for a second why I had gone outside.

"Molly, when are you going to learn to put your bike where . . ."

"Tad, quick, come here!" She was standing at the edge of the walk near the street, looking down at the three steps leading to the sidewalk. I saw her take a deep breath, winding up to scream again. I leaped forward.

"No. Don't yell, Molly. We heard you. Just don't yell!" She looked as if she were weighing the wisdom of just one more shrill wail for good measure. "No!" I repeated. Molly slowly exhaled, then looked down at her feet again.

She acted as if there was something blocking her way. I got a few steps closer and realized that something *was* blocking her way. This wasn't one of Molly's famous flights of fancy. Whatever was there, was real.

In the shadows cast by our old oak trees I couldn't see what had her all worked up. The faint glow of the street lights were no help.

At first glance, Molly's discovery looked like a big old sheep dog. Sort of white and black and fuzzy in spots.

"Picked up a stray, Molly?" My eyes were still adjusting to the dark and I couldn't tell. Molly didn't answer. She just giggled in apparent delight. "Something sure smells like a dog," I added.

"It's Santa Claus." Molly's tone was matter of fact and very I-told-you-so. I leaned over and took a deep whiff. The aroma almost knocked me over.

"Smells like a drunk dog if you ask me, Molly."

"Don't say that about Santa Claus, Tad." Molly could be a common scold when the occasion suited her. You'd think she was eleven years older than me instead of the other way around.

Of course, by this time the mystery—or part of it—had been solved. Our visitor—Molly's Santa Claus, my drunken sheep dog—was actually one of the street guys that wander around the alleys in the neighborhood. I even remembered seeing this fellow slicing open our plastic garbage bags and rooting around for aluminum cans and stuff. It had been a month or so before. I think he was one of the regulars. Sort of an unofficial member of the neighborhood association.

At first I was kind of scared. I didn't know if he was injured in a fight or sick or maybe even dead. Then I felt this sense of disgust. I mean, he did smell really bad. Then, and I'm ashamed to say only then, I realized he was just another two-legged animal like Molly and me—and in need.

He was thin and wiry, hardly enough meat on him to make anyone think he was Santa Claus. But he had a white beard and an old red overcoat and a dirty old Washington Redskins stocking cap pulled down over his head. Molly's got a great imagination. He could have been seventy or he could have been forty. Those guys must lead a pretty tough life and they tend to take on a timeless look about them. His hair was way past his collar, but didn't quite reach down to his shoulders. A sampling of his last couple of meals—solid and liquid—was matted in his beard. He was all curled up into a fetal position, and I finally sensed an aroma of cheap wine from his breath that assured me he wasn't dead.

He was definitely alive. The problem was that he had picked a bad time to camp out on our front steps. I don't suppose he ever watched television or listened to radio and I don't know if he ever read the newspaper. But I guess he didn't know that it was going to drop way below freezing and into the teens as the night went on.

We stared at him for a second or two together, then Molly stated very innocently, "Santa Claus is early, Tad."

"Yeah, well you see, Molly . . ."

"You think he wants some hot chocolate and cookies now?" She had cut me off in mid-sentence with what for her was a perfectly logical question. Molly doesn't fool around. She gets right to the heart of things.

"I think he's resting right now. Must have parked his reindeer down the street and thought he'd take a catnap here." I was kidding about the reindeer, but I saw Molly's eyes grow large. She believed me. She really did think it was Santa Claus. I started to backtrack and set things straight, but I couldn't think fast enough. Besides, what was I going to say? He's passed out on the front steps? He's three sheets to the wind? Santa Claus? Molly pressed her lips together, her devious mind spinning schemes.

"Why don't we wake him up and ask if he wants to go inside?"

That was all it would take to send Mom packing once and for all. She was always teetering on the edge anyway. Every time a jet flies in about forty feet from the top of our house, or the cars use our back alley for speed trials, or the apartment types park right in front of our house and take the only place Mom's got to unload groceries, Mom announces our retirement from urban pioneering. Imagine a bum on the front steps, invited into the house by her six-year-old daughter; Mom would get a real charge out of that all right.

"Hold on, Molly. Let's think about this before we do anything."

Molly stomped her foot down and stuck her chin out. Her big brother, the humbug, was no fun at all. In the meantime, I bit my lip and tried to think of what to do. I was drawing a total blank. If we left him out here much longer, he could die. If we tried to pick him up, he might get nasty on us. I mean he looked like he'd had a pretty rough life—scars on his face, a blackened eye, what looked like some gaps in his teeth peeking out from between his whiskers. If we told Mom, she would go bonkers. That only left us one choice; tell Dad and see what he had to say.

Now Molly is a little gullible, as if you couldn't tell from her thinking that some homeless guy was Santa Claus, but when it comes to dealing with Dad she's got a pretty good head about her. Dad had departed the kitchen and gone upstairs to his bathroom. We found him clean-shaven, dressed, and leaving a trail of Old Spice. Molly jumped into his arms and stretched the truth a little.

"Daddy . . . Daddy . . . something wonderful has happened, and we knew you'd know exactly what to do." I thought Molly was overplaying the "wisdom-of-the-father" angle, but Dad bought it. He's a sucker that way. He grinned, straightened up a little in paternal self-confidence, and stuck out his chin—just like Molly had a few minutes before. It was in the genes.

"You can always come to me, kids."

"Santa Claus is asleep on our steps, Daddy!" Molly blurted it out before I could build up to it a little more subtly.

Dad's eyes seemed to glaze over for a second. He must have thought we were playing some kind of trick on him.

"Well . . . uh . . . Dad . . . I think what Molly's saying is that there's this guy, you know, that looks kind of like Santa Claus." I gave Dad a big "let's-humor-the-child" wink and continued. "But whoever he really is, he's only got on an old overcoat . . . and he's asleep."

"Is this some kind of joke?" Dad's eyes had narrowed steadily as his suspicion about our motives grew.

"No," I added quickly, "there really is a guy out there."

"Well, we should invite him inside." Dad smiled, and swelled up with the spirit of the season.

"He smells really bad." I thought Dad deserved the truth up front if he was going to start feeling charitable.

"Yeah, he does," Molly seconded my observation.

"Well . . ." Dad moved his left palm across his mouth and let his index finger rest above his lip for a second. He was thinking through the same choices I had been through in my own mind. "We'll have to tell your mom first."

"He not only smells, but he's real dirty." I figured I might as well give him both barrels.

"Oh . . ." Dad was rethinking the wisdom of telling Mom right away. "Maybe I'd better have a look."

Dad and Molly and I hovered over our visitor like the three bears looking down at Goldilocks. I could see that Dad was taking the same mental notes I had made ten minutes before.

"Well," Dad finally ventured, "we've got to get him inside."

"All right!" Molly cheered Dad on and I stood trying to wish myself away from both of them.

"Tad, go get an old blanket from the front hall closet. We'll use it to get him inside."

I turned around, shivered with the increasing cold, and returned to the house. Just how, I wondered, were we three intrepid marvels of human salvation going to scoop our friend up and get him inside? I imagined various methods as I rummaged around in the closet for a blanket fit for service. I could grab his legs and Dad his arms, or vice versa, then carry him inside like a sack of cement. Or we could make a sling with our blanket instead of putting it over him. Or we could throw one of his arms around each of our shoulders and drag him inside with us. All of the alternatives had their flaws, not the least of which was avoiding his having an accident of one sort or another on us. I got outside with the blanket and placed my personal bet on the blanket as a sling.

"Tad, let's slide the blanket under him and we'll carry him in on top of it." Bingo. I was proud of myself as I worked with Dad to execute what was clearly the superior plan. I'll have to admit I felt a little guilty worrying about what the old guy might do to our clothes, but that didn't overcome my self-satisfaction. With Dad on two corners and me on the other two, we teetered up the front walk like *we* had been drinking or something. For a skinny little guy he sure weighed a lot. Maybe it was cold, or the fact that I was a little nervous. We opened the door and I could hear the hair dryer going. Mom was still oblivious to our guest.

We maneuvered Molly's Santa inside, put him on the front hall carpet, and covered him with the blanket. He slept through our grunting and groaning like a trooper. I stared across the inanimate figure of the ageless wanderer and smiled at Dad.

"Nice job," I said.

"Thanks." Dad took a deep breath.

"So, what's next?"

"What are you all doing downstairs?" The sound of Mom's dryer had ceased and her voice sounded like it was coming over an amplifier or something. Guilt. Fear. What would she say? Dad looked down, then around the hall and back at me. He was taking this adventure one step at a time.

"Nothing," Dad called. The whirling drone of the hair dryer started up again.

Dad turned back to me. "I don't think we have any choice. We'll have to call the police." Dad was talking in his low voice just in case Mom was faking us out. If the hair dryer's not going she can hear and immediately comprehend any sound in the house at any time of the night or day. Just ask me sometime when I've gotten home later than curfew.

"The police?" I was a little shocked. I mean, the guy hadn't really done anything wrong. "Why the police? I mean, why not the shelter? We're heading down there anyway." Like I said, Dad had made the Wayside Mission his special cause during the Christmas season. I figured Dad's first plan would be to drop the old guy off when we all went downtown.

"We can't take him to the shelter, he's been drinking."

"Well, of course he's been drinking," I blurted out.

"What's going on down there?" Mom's voice evidenced her growing suspicion.

"Nothing, Mom," I yelled, then continued in a hushed voice, "I thought all of these guys are winos or whatever."

Dad started to sugarcoat my rather blunt observation, but then he stopped in mid-sentence and started all over again. We weren't in public. We could say what was on our minds. It was just family.

"You're right," Dad began, "many of them do have alcohol problems. But in order to get into the front door of the mission, they have to be sober."

"Pretty tall order for some of those guys."

"But they manage it. For at least one meal a day. Our friend here would never pass the test." Dad nodded at our snoring Santa, Molly seated at his side, apparently unaware of or at least ignoring what we were saying. "So hopefully the police will come, take him to a nice warm cell, and let him sleep it off."

Dad was right. I hadn't thought it through yet, but I realized he was right. Dad made his way to the kitchen. Molly bounded up from her guard post, ran upstairs, and was back long before Dad, carrying one of the pillows from her bed.

"What's that for?" I knew but I was hoping I was wrong.

"For Santa's head, silly!" Molly looked at me with supreme disgust. What an insensitive dullard I must seem to my precocious baby sister. On the other hand, and in my defense, I was aware of the gallons of Clorox it would take to detoxify the pillow once the old guy had finished breathing into it. That's if the EPA didn't declare our whole house a hazardous waste site.

"Molly, maybe he likes sleeping on his arms."

"You are not serious!" Now she was really perturbed. Her big brother didn't have any sense whatsoever. She didn't wait, but put the pillow directly under his head. So much for those feathers! The old guy stirred, sunk his head into Molly's pillow with a contented sigh, and grabbed hold. A strange thought sprang briefly through my mind. In some other life, this guy had once slept on a pillow like Molly's every night.

"What shall we feed him?"

"Molly, this isn't a puppy or a kitten. He's a real guy, who's had a snoot full of Wild Irish Rose . . ."

"What's Wild Irish Rose?" Then before I could explain, "Santa drinks roses?"

"It's a wine, and look Molly, you might as well get this straight. This guy isn't Santa Claus."

Molly wasn't about to take my reassurance without a fight, but before she could respond Dad had emerged from the kitchen. He was scratching the bald spot on the crown of his head, just like he does when some project at work has got him stumped.

"Well?" I asked.

"The jails are full. Packed. And the one mission that'll take these guys when they're in their cups doesn't have any room either. I even checked at the Christian mission to see if I was wrong." Dad paused. "I was right."

"Then Santa's going to spend the night here!" Molly was ecstatic, exploding with the exclusivity of her discovery. She and she alone among her peers was the entrusted guardian of Santa Claus. As far as Dad and I were concerned, we were the reluctant innkeepers of a strung-out wino.

"He's not spending the night, Molly. Right, Dad?" I asked the question even while I knew there was probably no alternative. I hoped Dad had another idea, but I could tell by the way he was tearing at his eyebrow that he didn't know either.

"Right, Tad." Dad nodded with an assurance that I knew he didn't really believe. "At least until, or unless, he wakes up. Then he's on his own." Good idea, Dad. Once he was up, he was out.

"Right, Dad. Got it, Molly?" I sounded a lot more certain than I felt. Bold talk, big words. But we were in a pickle, plain and simple. We couldn't plop him back on our front steps. He'd die. It was getting colder out there all the time. I had this sudden, goofy image of the police slapping handcuffs on Dad and me—and little, dinky handcuffs on Molly—while Mom watched, horrified, from the top of the stairs. "I'm sorry, but this is manslaughter," or maybe, "Save your explanations for the prosecutor, this is Murder Two." No. Cut it out. Think straight, I told myself. The point was that no matter how bad he smelled, old Clarence or Freddie or Godfrey or whoever he was, was another human being. Having taken him in, we couldn't take him back out. We were committed to his short-term future. We'd bought into it, wittingly or not. He had adopted us, or our front yard, and now we had adopted him.

"So, what do we do, Daddy?" Molly looked at Dad with those sickening big brown eyes and thick heavy eyelashes, batting convincingly with the rhythms of the moment. I swear Molly was going to drive guys nuts some day.

Just as Dad was going to answer, Mom decided to swish down the front stairs in her best, dress-up-to-go-serve-in-the-soup-kitchen sweater and slacks. She was halfway down before she realized exactly what, if not precisely who, was lying in her front hall. She didn't scream. She didn't faint. She didn't start asking questions a mile a minute. She was calm, all things considered.

"Brought home another client from the office, dear?" I thought that was a pretty good line, considering the circumstances, and I started laughing hysterically. Dad shot me a dirty look.

"Tad and Molly found this fellow on our front stoop." Dad's voice was very deep, his words well-modulated. "And we brought him in out of the cold. And the police can't take him." Dad's explanation began to run together and his words started tumbling out of his mouth like popcorn. "And the mission won't take him and none of the other missions have room and so he's here and I don't know what we can do . . ."

It's pitiful watching Dad when he's in a state of fluster. Sometimes Mom jumps in and helps him out. This time she let him go on for a few more seconds. Then she held up her hand and the jumble stopped. A moment's silence. That all-important instant when no one knows whether Mom will let us have it or reason us out of crisis. She was being cool about the whole thing. Too cool considering the fact that our visitor was overwhelming the smell of "forest pine" candles that had been doing a pretty good job of giving the front hall that "woodsy" aroma just a few minutes before. And then there was the matter of the rug in the front hall. Dad had given it to Mom as part of her birthday present just two weeks before. For the first time that I could remember, we were supposed to take off our shoes when we came in the house! This carpet was going to last or we would have to pay! So "cool" wasn't necessarily a good sign. Then she began to speak.

"You and Tad and Molly did the right thing." I breathed a sigh of major relief and as I looked at Dad I noticed his shoulders relax and his smile return. Salvation. "And obviously we can't turn him out into the cold." At this Molly started jumping up and down in obvious anticipation of telling everybody at Kennedy Elementary that she—a lowly first-grader—had hosted Santa Claus. "So someone has to stay here with him until he wakes up . . . and then . . ." Even Mom didn't have a ready answer for what would happen then. ". . . and then we'll just have to see what to do next."

"Then it's settled," Dad noted calmly. "You all go on to the mission and I'll stay here."

Ordinarily this would be a logical solution. Dad usually gets stuck with the short-term nasty tasks—Mom gets the long-term. But this time obvious logic failed, at least as far as I was concerned. Dad was the one who had started getting our church interested in the mission downtown. We had done duty over Thanksgiving on a sort of trial basis. Now the big challenge was getting the congregation there for Christmas. He had worked out the details with our minister, made the announcements for three Sundays in a row, and generally twisted everybody's arms to join us. Not that they didn't want to head down to the mission the week before Christmas—but without my dad's pestering them they just wouldn't. Everybody gets busy, and then there's no time. Besides, some of them hadn't been downtown after dark in years. So for Dad not to keep his own date with the mission wouldn't be a good idea. No one would believe that one of these guys had actually fallen asleep in our front hall. We'd have to take pictures or get sworn affidavits from the Melrose sisters or something.

On the other hand, I'd only been lukewarm about the whole mission deal. Not that I minded the service part—it was just that I felt so useless. The adults hustled around doing the right thing with the plates and the silverware and the food and stuff while I felt like a fifth wheel. I mean, all I did at Thanksgiving was get in everybody's way until everything was done better and quicker than I could have done it myself. So here was my chance to go AWOL and help Dad out in the process. I never pretended to be noble—but it sure was convenient to be big-hearted.

"Wait, Dad. You can't stay here. You're chairman—everybody expects to see you. But I on the other hand . . . Why, our old buddy there . . ."

"Santa Claus . . ." Molly interrupted.

"Whoever," I continued, "when he wakes up, he's not going to hurt anybody. I'll give him some soup and a sandwich and then he can . . ." I puzzled for an instant over exactly where he would go. I guess I never had thought about it before. "Well, he can either go or stay until you guys get home. Then we can take him to the mission together. He'll be sober enough to pass the test." I was waxing eloquent in my overflowing nobility. What a great guy I was. I even surprised myself.

Dad thought about my proposition for a second or so, then turned to Mom. She nodded her approval.

"Okay, Tad. I think you can handle anything that happens. And you've got the phone number for the mission and the police."

"Sure, Dad. No problem." I was really at my chivalric best.

"And I'm staying too!" Molly had been quiet too long.

"No, you're not!"

"Yes, I am."

"No, you're not!"

"Tad . . . Molly . . . stop it." I was glad Dad interceded. When Molly gets on to something there's no blasting her loose. Then

Dad threw me for a real loop. "If Molly wants to stay, she can stay."

"Come on, Dad." It was bad enough baby-sitting the neighborhood derelict, but Molly too? This was cruel and unusual punishment.

"Tad, I'll pay you . . . double." Dad had me. I needed the cash for car insurance.

"Okay. But you guys have to tell her that when I say to bed, I mean to bed."

"Fair enough, Tad." Dad turned around to get his coat. They were already late.

"Tad," Mom's voice had that ominous hesitation about it that always makes me nervous. It was like the part on the old "Candid Camera" show where the host shows the dupes how dumb they've been and they're supposed to be polite about it. She cleared her throat. "You ought to know that Sarah Jane is supposed to be volunteering at the mission tonight with her parents."

Talk about a bombshell! Sarah Jane and I had broken up at the end of sophomore year. For the whole first half of junior year I had been trying to figure a way to mend the error of my ways—which to be honest about it, was a matter of overcoming Sarah Jane's crush on this senior guy. I had been looking for some excuse to do something with Sarah Jane again. A church function was perfect! Now Mom had let me go on like Mother Theresa or something until I had dug myself in too deep to get out. I guess it wasn't on purpose, I just hadn't stopped talking. But what was I going to say: "Take it back, Dad. Just kidding. Nobody'll miss you!"?

I started to quote Dickens' "'tis a far, far better thing I do . . ." but I settled for, "No . . . Sarah Jane or no Sarah Jane, Dad should be down at the mission with you and I should stay here with Sleeping Beauty . . ."

"Santa Claus . . ." Molly piped in.

"Okay . . . okay."

I couldn't believe what I was saying. I mean, I'm not that selfless. I'm not that self-centered either, but in matters of the heart, my informed self-interest usually overcomes altruism. Not this time. It must have been Christmas.

"No, you go on. Just say hello to Sarah Jane for me."

Mom and Dad assured me they would acknowledge my existence to Sarah Jane, then they threw their coats on and left. The front door slammed shut and we were alone. Molly looked at me and smiled. The supremely innocent crescent-moon smile of a child who knows no fear. She was beside herself in six-year-old satisfaction.

I, on the other hand, was beginning to have second thoughts. As long as Mom and Dad had been there, everything was fine. I had seen the fellow around—out in the alley or walking down the street with that glazed-over, eyes-ahead stare. He always seemed harmless enough outside of our house. But now he was *inside.* And except for Molly, who was in an ecstatic delirium, I was alone. I guess you think about things one way with all of your family around you, and another with a sweet but pixilated six-year-old.

Molly and I went into the kitchen. I fixed a ham and swiss sandwich and Molly poured a glass of milk. (I convinced her that hot chocolate would get cold while he napped.) Molly situated herself on the bottom step of the stairway, her elbows implanted on her knees, her chin set within her palms. The girl was not about to budge. Not to watch the television, not to play a rip-roaring game of Candyland, not to go play dolls in the big closet in her room. And I sure couldn't leave the hallway while a guy, who my imagination had transformed from Freddie the Freeloader to a mass murderer, was lying there ready to wake up and wreak mayhem. So there we were. Molly with her Santa carefully snoozing away on her pillow. I with my crazed killer trying to deceive me with the cadence of his snoring.

"Tad?"

"What Molly?"

"What if Santa doesn't wake up? What if he's sick? He really doesn't look too good." Now she was noticing our charge's state of health! I didn't have much choice but to reassure her.

"Well, whoever he is, I think he'll be okay as soon as he sleeps it off a little."

Molly paused. I could tell she was mulling over something that wasn't going to be easy for me to address.

"Do you believe in Santa Claus?" Great, the ultimate question. The one only parents are supposed to tackle. I thought hard, and fast. If I waited too long to answer I might give her the wrong idea.

"Yes, I do."

"Have you ever seen Santa before tonight?" She was obviously sticking to the weightiness of our discovery.

"No . . . but I know the, uh, spirit of Christmas has been alive for a long, long time. And I don't think it could have lasted this long if it . . . or rather, if Santa wasn't real." I was holding my own. Now, if she would just go on to something else. I knew this was wishful thinking.

"Then why don't you believe he's Santa?" She nodded toward our friend.

"Well . . . I don't know. I mean, you usually expect to see Santa a little more in charge of things . . . what with the reindeer and his sack of toys and coming down the chimney and all. And this guy seems a little skinny for old St. Nick." I was reverting to my own childhood fantasies of how Santa should appear.

"You don't really believe Santa comes down the chimney, do you?" Molly asked. Now who was challenging whom? Molly was a sharp kid—for all of her shortcomings—and I wondered where she was headed.

"I don't know. If he wants to come down a chimney, I guess he can."

"And it would be easier for a skinny guy to come down a chimney than a fat guy, wouldn't it?"

"Well, I guess so."

"And if he wanted to dress up in old clothes and smell like . . ." I knew she was trying to remember.

"Wild Irish Rose?"

"Yeah . . . if he wanted to smell like that, he could, couldn't he?"

"I suppose so. It's just that that's not how I expect him to make his debut appearance on our street." I was trying to be funny, but Molly didn't get it.

"People didn't expect Jesus to be born in a manger with a bunch of stinky animals, did they?"

"Well, no. Actually, they were expecting something on a little grander scale."

"Okay!" She had me. I was getting sucked in and her six-year-old logic was winning. "So, what if like Jesus, Santa wanted to surprise us. What if he wanted to see what we would give *him* for a change?"

I was stumped. In the space of two minutes Molly had stripped me of my most studied seventeen-year-old sophistication. I even felt a little chill. The kind when you realize that something is happening that you can't really explain. It ran from my shoulders down to my toes, then back again to my shoulders where it hovered for a while. She had me wondering just who this guy *really* was. Wondering with no better answers than those Molly had provided.

"Well," I thought maybe a few specifics might help us both out, "if he wakes up, I'm going to give him something to eat for starters."

"His ham sandwich and milk?"

"Well, yeah, and maybe some cookies, if he's still hungry."

"Okay." Molly gave me long, relaxed yawn. Somewhere in the devious maze-like passages of Molly's brain, her questions had been answered—at least in part. "Wake me up if I can help." And with that, Molly left her post, crawled down on the rug next to me, and put her head in my lap. All my past and future complaints about my little sister dissolved in their own insignificance. She probably hadn't thought a thing about it. She was just a little worn out after the excitement of the last hour. Besides, it was past eight and almost Molly's bedtime. She was at peace. She was secure in the answers of the moment. And she thought my lap was soft and warm. She snuggled in to get more comfortable, murmured something with the word "love" in it, and fell asleep.

Now completely alone—except for two peaceful sleepers—I stared in silence at Molly's Santa. The crevices in his face looked as if someone had cut them years before—deep and meant to last forever. Not scars really. More like notches to mark the places he'd been and the experiences he'd had. Souvenirs of life. His beard wasn't fluffy or fanciful or anything like the Coke commercials. His was thick and white, and besides being matted, just plain weathered. Like him, it had been through a lot.

I wondered whether in some prior life, some life he had fled years before, he had served duty as Santa Claus for another little girl like Molly. If he had, where was she today? Did she know where her Santa was tonight? Did she know where her Santa was most other nights? Did she have her own Molly by now? Mystery that he was, he could have had any of a thousand lives that I could imagine there in the silence of my own childhood home. His past could hold marvelous stories, or could hold nothing but sorrow and a compulsion to escape. Maybe like Molly I was getting sleepy, a little stressed by the evening or spooked by the quiet that, for a change, possessed our home. But funny thoughts started to spin around in my head.

Who decided that Santa lived at the North Pole? Had that all been made up to make us feel better? To give the old fellow *somewhere* he could call home? And what if that was why he visited all of us, skipping from one place to the next, always leaving more behind than he took with him. What if he was wandering in search of "home"—not a specific home, or place, but the spirit of home, of belonging? What if it was that quality—the quality of home—that he helped reinvest in the lives of anyone who would open up to him?

I don't know why everything about Christmas seemed so real with him lying there and me, with Molly in my lap and nowhere to go, sitting with them in the hallway. Maybe it was just the quiet—the incredible, freeing quiet of nowhere else to be but home. Now I'm a pretty thoughtful guy. I make pretty good grades and all that. But around this time of year I get moving so fast that by the time I think about the meaning of Christmas and giving gifts and sharing times together, the holidays have passed. This evening I didn't have any choice.

I must have sat there for another hour or more. My eyes started to water. It was too bright. I reached up, flipped off the switch to the hall light, and was instantly immersed in the soft glow of Mom's thick, scented candles on the coat rack. "Silent night. Holy night." My eyes started blinking. My companions' drowsiness was contagious. The last thing I remember was thinking how funny it was to feel myself breathing slower and slower as I finally gave up trying to keep my eyes open.

The clock on the living room mantle went off and my eyes popped open. How long had I been asleep? It was just past eight when I turned off the overhead light. I tried to count the gongs, including the first one which woke me up. Nine? Yes, it had to be. Mom and Dad were supposed to be home by ten. I started to recap the strange events of the evening, my mind jump starting into high gear pretty quickly. Then I noticed. Things were different. Something had changed. I turned my head and I realized what was different. Molly's Santa was sitting upright on the blanket, his eyes open, fixed dreamily on me.

I started to say something but he stopped me, raising his bony finger to his lips and nodding slightly toward Molly. He didn't want to wake her. I smiled. The sudden start of adrenalin which had begun racing through me when I first saw him awake now disappeared. He apparently wasn't going to spend the night on the front carpet either. But what was he going to do?

The old guy drew the threadbare sleeve of his crummy overcoat across his mouth and burped. I was silently thankful for the scent of Mom's candles. Then he moved his tongue around inside his mouth and looked as if he was remembering that his last meal had been the last part of somebody's bottle of wine. I picked up the plate holding the sandwich I had made for him and extended it toward him. I was still bound by Molly's head and shoulders. He was still bound by what must have been one humdinger of a headache. He took the sandwich, winked at me, and started munching away. While he did, he looked around him. I could see that he was trying to figure out just how he had wound up in our front hall. I started to tell him, then I stopped. Ours probably wasn't the first home he had awakened to in his years of wandering. It probably wouldn't be the last. He looked as if he already understood anything I could have attempted to explain. So I didn't try.

He polished off the sandwich and started to get up. I offered him the lukewarm milk, and to my considerable surprise he drank it. For a second he stood there, just staring down at Molly. His eyes were a watery blue, but not teary. I'm not sure whether he had any tears left. His features never changed, the creases never spread or broke or dissolved into a smile or frown. I thought at first he was still a little hazy from all the cheap wine, but then I changed my mind as I noticed the way his eyes absorbed every detail.

When he had taken it all in, he nodded again, as if to say yes, then he slipped his right hand into the pocket of his old Harpo Marx overcoat and slowly drew it out again. He took a step toward us, then went down on one knee next to Molly's head. His gnarled fist loosened to reveal a heavy, old-fashioned chrome whistle. The kind Mr. King the gym teacher claims he got when he was a little boy in the fifties. It hung from a green and gold, plastic woven chain. The old guy fitted it gingerly around Molly's neck, touched her once, lightly, on the cheek with his finger, then stood up. He started for the door.

I wanted to stop him. I wanted to tell him to spend the night. I wanted to explain where the guest room was and the towels and the soap and all of that stuff, but I knew that it wouldn't do any good. He was going somewhere. Maybe he didn't know where or why or how he was going to get there. But he was headed out. He would always be headed out. Always roaming from one home's doorstep and back alley to another—until death or something bigger and more influential than me would halt his wandering. I couldn't stop him. But I could do something.

"Wait," I whispered. Molly stirred, but didn't awaken.

He turned and looked down at me. I eased Molly's head over slightly until both arms were free. The ball inside her chrome whistle jiggled. Then with one swift move I slipped off the big old ski sweater I was wearing.

"Here. You're going to need this," I said. He looked at it for a second, wondering, or so I imagined, whether he should take it. Santa usually restricts himself to consumables. Then without a word, and as quick and slick as can be, he dropped his overcoat around his knees, glided my sweater over his head, and reaching down, brought his overcoat back up around him. Then, before I could say anything else, he opened the door and was gone.

Now I was truly alone—even though Molly slept contentedly in my lap. In the corner of the hallway, like a teenage Buddha, I sat as still as the house itself. I wanted to do something. Call someone. Tell someone what had happened. I wanted to shake Molly lightly until she woke up. Then I wanted to pour my feelings out upon my six-year-old sister. I touched her hair lightly, then stopped. The soft glow of candlelight caught the silverish gleam of the whistle that rested on the folds of her hair. I picked it up and held it close to my eyes where I could see it better. It was smooth and worn in places, but even in the dimness I could make out a fragment of an inscription: "To Betty, From Dad. Christmas 1959."

Its history would never be revealed. I would never learn about Betty or Dad or the Christmas of 1959. Neither would Molly. Maybe it had belonged to Betty's Santa in another life. Maybe Molly's Santa had found it in a Goodwill store. But now it was Molly's— once I cleaned it in boiling water and convinced Mom and Dad that it was okay. Molly wore it proudly and kept it safely hidden away when it wasn't about her neck.

For a while I didn't see him around the neighborhood. Then after a few months we bumped into each other in the back alley one night when I was taking out the garbage. We looked into each other's eyes and he registered recognition. Then he nodded. It was March and cold and he was wearing my sweater and I was glad.

Angel Tree

Angel Tree

IN THE END, the joke was on me and the tragedy of my Christmas Eve was amusing—sort of. But that's not how it began. In the beginning it was grim and getting worse by the minute. Neither Cassandra nor I were laughing. I reached for that crummy little card on the Angel Tree and plucked it from the branch.

"You see," I must have growled, "I can think of someone besides myself."

"That doesn't prove a thing," she countered. Cassandra's first year with the county attorney's office had given her a prosecutor's perspective on life. Everyone was on trial. Every truth subject to proof.

"I don't need to prove anything." I shoved the card in my suit pocket and kept on walking down the main mall corridor.

"Then you don't need to take a card when it doesn't mean anything." She pushed her dark-blue fashion glasses up against the bridge of her nose and quickened her pace. Cassandra does that when we disagree—we had disagreed a good bit during the past few weeks. Then her voice becomes cold and professional—"Ms. Prosecutor." When it warms up, I know she's ready to forgive my transgressions.

"I don't need to do anything I don't want to do," I said.

She stopped, turning sharply. "That's fair, Fred. Fair for you and

131

fair for me. So I don't think we need to go Christmas shopping together . . . especially since you don't seem to be in the mood."

She had me there. I wasn't in the mood. I had called her that afternoon to suggest dinner. She suggested Christmas shopping beforehand and I said okay. That was my mistake. Christmas was fine for children and partying and people in retail, but ever since I was a little kid I hadn't been overwhelmed by it all. Rushing around buying shirts and blouses and skirts and pants; pens, watches, rings, and books that no one reads was not my idea of time well spent.

We walked on in silence, staring in the windows of the shopping mall stores. The Gap, The Limited, B. Dalton's, and even The Nature Company dulled me to the core. I took a minor interest in the performance of their stocks on the New York Exchange, but as far as I was concerned I could have been in Hoboken or Omaha. The stores were all stamped out of some architects' manual back in corporate headquarters—the same from one city to another. That was not the point, Cassandra had told me earlier, but since I didn't seem to get the point, I was probably beyond salvation. Cassandra didn't even window shop. The woman was seriously burned.

I knew what was bothering her. She had a veritable cornucopia of the Christmas spirit and I could barely muster a "Merry Christmas." From the moment we got out of the car I countered her every word of cheer and goodwill and peace on earth with a quip about the strategies behind retail sales or the increases in gang shootings. It had been like that for weeks.

"Look," I finally broke our silence with my closest approximation of an apology, "I'm sorry for whatever I said."

"You said that it didn't matter what I got my father, or what I got for you or you me or what anyone did for anyone else."

"Well, I did say something like that . . ."

"You said that the only thing anybody really cared about was the price of the 'item.'"

"Well, in a symbolic way, that's what I said . . . sure." I fumbled, repeating my error of moments earlier. "Isn't that it?"

Cassandra stopped. I stopped. We were right in front of the World Bazaar. How perfect, I thought. Even before it happened I had the surreal sense that we were about to break up in front of the very store where we had met that past spring. What had Cassandra seen in me then that was now so hideously contorted with the coming of Christmas?

"No," she said, "what counts is that you're giving gifts out of love . . . whether it's to honor Christ or fellowship or humanity or just plain decency."

"Then why don't we just make it simple—write out a check to your favorite charity and be done with it?"

"You *would* boil it all down to money, wouldn't you?"

"It's simpler."

"Is that the point? Make it simple?"

"Well, it would make fewer people depressed after Christmas. I mean, no build-up, no let-down."

"No highs? No lows? Is that it?"

"I'm not advocating it . . . I just said it would be simpler." What I was not telling her—what I couldn't tell her because I wasn't fully aware of it myself—was that I had my own reasons for circumventing the hoopla. I had lived with anticipation and disappointment before.

Cassandra looked at me. Lord, she was beautiful. Tall and athletic, boldly brunette with sharp, pronounced features. They were even more pronounced as we stood there in front of the World Bazaar. She was a competitor, just like me. And, like me, she said what was on her mind. Her lips were set in a line just as straight as her jaw and I knew she was about to say something I was not supposed to forget.

"Fred, I used to think we had a lot of things in common. Same sports, same books, same movies. But I had no idea your view of the world was so hard—so cut and dried."

"My view's not hard, it just doesn't soften like butter between Thanksgiving and New Year's—like some people."

"I want to go home."

"Look, let's just grab some dinner. We can talk it over and get past all of this. I mean, I don't even know how this goofy argument started." And I still didn't know. One minute we were two happily consenting adults walking through a typical American shopping mall. The next, we were on the verge of breaking up.

"I'm going to call a cab. I'll talk to you later." She turned and started to leave. Then she looked over her shoulder. "I take that back. If you ever figure out what the Christmas spirit means, I'll talk to you. Good-bye, Fred."

She was gone. I was alone. Abandoned in a wasteland of endless chain stores. I watched her walk to the Baskin-Robbins, then turn down a side corridor toward the public phones. There wasn't any use following her. It was over. So I stood like some misplaced sandbar in the middle of a steady flow of Christmas shoppers. They parted from their course to avoid running over me, but I was simply a bother. I didn't catch any sympathetic glances. Most of them looked down or away. And I didn't see any glimmer of the

Christmas spirit in their eyes. If I hadn't found it, neither had they. But that was little consolation.

Benefit plans are my business. The legal deduction and the sheltered income are my business. Vesting, funding, and growing employee contributed pensions are my business. I am an accountant and an actuary and damned good at it. Three of the biggest plans in the city are mine to manage. I am, by most accounts, a bright, aggressive young man moving up in a tough world. I'm also generous—at least, I think so. I take my clients to lunch, provide them basketball tickets whenever possible, and there's always a box available at the track. So what was Cassandra so upset about?

Christmas Eve. I sat in front of my computer monitor, trying to concentrate on three new 401(k)s that had to be ready before the Christmas break. The front desk was holding my calls and I had canceled two final business appointments and a haircut. I should have been happily immersed in massaging contribution levels, but instead I was befuddled more than ever by Cassandra.

Our scene in the mall had been building since Thanksgiving. It hadn't taken much reflection to figure that out. Every week there had been something that grated on us. The first week it was the old movies. Not just any old movies, but old black-and-white Christmas movies. Cassandra and I liked to watch movies on the weekend— we'd pop popcorn, curl up, and enjoy. But the weekend after Thanksgiving she rented some movie about an old man who thinks he's Santa Claus—calls himself Kris Kringle. I'd heard about it, but never seen it. It was okay. Pretty corny, but a total fantasy. Cassandra cried and I started thinking about what it was like when I was a little kid thinking that Santa was coming. She could tell I was less than thrilled.

She tried again with that "It's a Great Life" movie. That was when I tried to make a joke: "Potter's not so bad," I chuckled, "he keeps his shareholders happy and that Bailey fellow runs the type of thrift that almost brought the country down a few years ago." Cassandra laughed but I could tell she was thinking of something else. I asked her.

"My daddy and I stayed up one night and watched that movie before there was cable—before everyone knew about it." She paused. "My daddy cried with me."

Again, at the time, I didn't know why I said it, but it came out automatically. "Well, I've always wondered why everyone raves about it."

You would have thought she had stock in the old film. She

frowned, munched her popcorn, sipped some wine, and changed the subject.

The next weekend she asked me to go to church. The First Sunday in Advent, she said. I declined, thanking her, but opting instead for the forty-ninth Sunday with the *New York Times*. I offered to take her out for brunch afterwards but she wasn't interested. I should have just told her the truth—that my parents didn't go to church and sure didn't encourage me to go; that Advent services or Christmas services or any type of church service was pretty foreign to me. Instead I made my little joke.

The next week she invited me to help trim her family's tree. I started to say yes, then backed away, fearing another bad scene. I made some excuse about work at the office; a few days later I asked her out on our ill-fated dinner date.

I should have seen it all coming. I should have remembered back on how sparse Christmas was around my house. Cassandra was a Christmas person. I wasn't. Cassandra carried childhood memories of one special experience after another; moments that built to a crescendo until Christmas itself. Older brothers returning from college, a father who watched those Christmas movies with her, a mother who read Christmas stories to the whole family even after they were all grown. I didn't have any of that.

I'll give you an example of what Christmas was for me. It was a real stand-out. I was about six. My dad was a facts and figures man of his day—just like I am now. He was chief financial officer for one of the big companies in town. Anyway, I made my list for Santa Claus. I should have waited and given it to Mom, but I was anxious. Even if we weren't church-goers we celebrated Christmas—at least I got presents. And I had just finished my list for Santa Claus. I gave it to Dad one Saturday morning as he was passing my room. He was on his way to the office. Dad smiled, said he'd send it on to Santa, and slipped it in his pocket.

The weeks before Christmas were full of the same type of anticipation that so many people still seem to experience as adults—at least Cassandra does. Time seems forever when you're six. I had to keep asking *when* Christmas was actually going to come. All of the days seemed to fold into each other like so many nesting bowls.

When Christmas morning came, I rushed downstairs. The lights of the tree were already on. Santa had been there. No doubt about it. But there had been a mistake. Nothing that I had asked for was there. There was an adequate quantity of other toys which I was sure belonged to some other boy. But they weren't mine. Santa had gotten his orders mixed up.

When my parents came downstairs a minute later, they must have read the look on my face. They asked what was wrong. I talked around the problem for a few seconds, then told them. My mother put her arm around me. My father had the look of guilt—eyebrows raised, head nodding, lips pouted. I could tell right away: he had forgotten to mail my list to Santa Claus and the jolly old elf had left whatever extra toys he had lying around. Christmas was never quite the same after that for me.

Now my parents live in Arizona. We always call on Christmas. I used to go out there for a few days the last week of December. My dad and I never speak about his Christmas oversight—probably because we've both forgotten about it. At least I had until Cassandra left me in the mall. During the next two weeks I had time to think about a lot of things—my lack of Christmas spirit included. Maybe it was just that one incident that stood out in my mind. Maybe it was a combination of things. Maybe there were other events that I still haven't remembered. But I resolved that *if* Cassandra and I ever saw each other again I would try to talk through my Christmas phobia with her.

So there I was on Christmas Eve: alone in the office, drinking Diet Coke like it was mother's milk, and punching away at the keyboard to paste together the right figures with the right clauses. I wanted to call Cassandra. I knew I couldn't concentrate on anything until I did. Someone had to be working at the county attorney's office, even if it was Christmas Eve. Cassandra was low person on the totem pole—maybe it was her. I picked up the phone, dialed her direct number, and hung up after the first ring. I did the same thing time and again. I couldn't go through with it, but I couldn't keep myself from trying.

In between calls I kept plugging away at those 401(k)s. And every time I would think I was conquering some intricate detail, Cassandra would pop into my head and all of the intricate details would dissipate into a jumble of words. I stood up, walked around, opened drawers into old files, and fidgeted away one minute after another. I finally flipped on the radio—something I never do at work—just to get my mind on something else. It was almost five and I thought I might catch the close of the market. Instead I got the funny afternoon disc jockey. That was okay. He always made me laugh when I drove home at night. I turned it up. He was doing the lead into an old Christmas song. I listened and felt even lonelier.

Why was the actual arrival of Christmas such a downer? Even for an unspirited Scrooge like me? Why did I always treat Christmas like it could be avoided, knowing that it couldn't? Why hadn't I made some plans for Christmas Eve and Christmas Day if I wasn't going to see Cassandra? I had friends. Not everyone had wives or significant others. Not everyone went back home to their parents. Other guys I knew did things. I wasn't sure what, but they did something. Someone would have taken me in if I had dropped a hint or two. But now it was too late.

The song ended and the disc jockey started talking again.

"Okay, shoppers, your time's up. The big push is over . . . well, almost over. I mean, you could count the last six hours, but if you haven't done it yet, you're in a heap of trouble . . ." He went on for a few more minutes before I zeroed in on what he was saying. ". . . so for you sinners who took a card and screwed up—shame on you. The River Mall folks tell us that ninety-nine percent of the Angel Tree wishes have been fulfilled . . . but for you other one percent out there who have let some little child down—hah, you ought to be 'boiled with your own pudding, and buried with a stake of holly through your heart.'"

Every inch of me chilled. My pulse soared and my breath started coming in little starts. I got up, went to my suit pocket and reached in. It was still there. I had worn the same suit that night with Cassandra at the mall. And it was into the right-hand pocket of that suit that I had buried, unexamined, the Angel Tree wish card.

I unfolded the piece of paper. I was part of the one percent. One of the slobs who didn't care enough to follow up on a simple commitment. Suddenly Christmas wasn't just between me and my past, or me and Cassandra, or even me and the rest of the world. It was between me and some kid that I had never met. And whether he was going to have a gizillion presents from every other charity in town, and whether he was tomorrow's gang killer or basketball star, I had been bold enough to pluck his number and his wish from the Angel Tree.

And all he was, was a number. Number 711 to be exact. And what did he want? He wanted a fire truck. A simple, classic kid's gift. I didn't know how old he was. Couldn't be too old to want a fire truck. But it specified a pump and a siren. Old enough to know what he wanted. Just like me at six. What could I do? If the disc jockey was right, I was too late.

Another Christmas song was playing. Maybe the disc jockey would have an idea. He was bound to know something. I dug into my phone book and punched in the number to the station.

"I need to talk to Harry," I told the receptionist.

"He's on the air right now; if you'll leave your name . . ."

"I know he's on the air. I just heard him talking about the Angel Tree. I'm the one percent. I need to find out what I can do," I persisted, pulling name, title, instances in which Harry Majors and I had been at the same awards banquet, people we knew in common—anything. I was relentless and finally the receptionist was relenting. I waited another minute on hold, then he was on the line.

"Okay," his voice dripping with sarcasm, "so I'm talking to one of the reprobates!"

"Yes . . . guilty. Can you tell me who to talk to, if there's something I can do."

He paused. I could tell he was looking for something. That gave me hope.

"Okay, it's probably too late, but try this number . . . Interfaith Charities. Ask for Sister Pat Monahan. She's the one who calls here with updates and so on."

I thanked him, hung up, and punched the numbers in for Interfaith Charities. It rang three . . . six . . . nine times. Of course it was too late. It was almost six o'clock. The office was bound to be closed. I was condemned to slobdom.

"Hello, Interfaith Charities."

I couldn't believe someone had actually answered. It didn't matter if I had the archbishop or the night watchman, it was a voice. I asked for Sister Pat. He knew who she was, but she'd already left. I asked if anyone there had the list that matched numbers with names. The man was polite but couldn't help. The list was with Sister Pat. And where was she? Probably at Holy Spirit, he answered, getting ready for Christmas Eve Mass.

He gave me the number, I thanked him, punched another free line on my phone—no time to hang up—and tapped the numbers out for Holy Spirit. My finger slipped and I tried again. Three rings later I found out I had dialed the wrong number. I must have transposed a four and a five. I sat back and took a breath. I was about to hyperventilate and that wouldn't help anything.

I tried again, someone answered "Holy Spirit," and I asked for Sister Pat. I was quizzed on who was calling, what I wanted, why I couldn't wait until the day after Christmas, and a dozen other questions. I straggled through my oral exams and was finally put on hold. Minutes passed—then a voice.

"This is Sister Pat. Can I help you?"

I explained my dilemma. She listened politely.

"There are other people in your situation who never call us. I appreciate that you called. But just go off and be with your family. Relax, that little boy isn't going to go without Christmas. We have extra gifts that we buy with donations. He'll get something."

"But he may not get what he wanted."

"That's true. But in life we don't get everything we ask for. Don't worry about it."

"But I will worry about it. I'm already going crazy about it. I promise you I have nothing better to do."

"We don't personalize our gifts. We don't want to underscore any division between the haves and have nots."

"I'll make sure no one sees me. I'll drop the gift at the front door. Promise."

She hesitated, started to reiterate Interfaith's policy, then stopped.

"I tell you what, Fred. Who am I to squelch the Christmas spirit? I'll give you the address and boy's first name. I don't know where you're going to find a toy fire truck at this hour, but good luck. If you don't, don't worry. We'll take care of it later."

She gave me his name and address—Jamal, at 543 Highland—I thanked her again and hung up.

Up to this point, I hadn't thought twice about why I was so frantic. I simply kept moving and talking through one phone call after another. Now, for an instant before I turned out the office lights, gathered up my overcoat, and started my search, I had to ask myself whether I was really nuts. Even if I found the fire truck, I knew Jamal's neighborhood wasn't safe after dark. Sister Pat was probably right. And as Cassandra recognized, I'm not a natural for Christmas. So why do it?

Answers flew through my head. First off, Jamal and I had a contract of sorts. I had all but breached it and the least I could do was try to make it right. Then there was the matter of the gift itself. Sister Pat could rationalize all she wanted to, but Jamal would be disappointed—just as Cassandra was already disappointed—and I didn't need to disappoint anyone else this Christmas. The simplest reason was that *I* felt crummy and I knew I'd feel better if I did what I said I'd do. My last reason for going out was the strangest of all. In a way I was trekking out on Christmas Eve for the sake of my dad. You see, back when I was six there had been a fire truck on my wish list too. If Dad had discovered his mistake in time, he would have done something about it. I know he would. He's basically a decent guy. Trying was the least I could do—for him and for me.

My attack on the shopping malls was a bust. By eight o'clock I figured out that the toy stores had all closed at six. The department stores as well. Nothing seemed open. I rode up and down the main strips looking for any place that was open. The streets were as empty at eight as they had been gorged with people just six hours before. So I found myself doing circles in the parking lot of a Toys Я Us. Round and round, trying to figure out which way to go next. Another mall in the south end? Farther east?

Four circles completed it came to me—I should have started around the corner from my condo. That's where the extra-large, all-night Walgreen had opened a few months before. It had toys— I remembered seeing them. I straightened my car out and headed back toward downtown and home.

With no traffic I was there in just a few minutes. I found myself bathed in unflattering fluorescence, sharing the aisles with delin-quent dads from all over the city. There must have been a dozen of them, barely acknowledging each other, eyes glassy, all singly directed to the slim pickings on the toy shelves.

At first I thought I was out of luck. There wasn't much in the way of trucks left, and I surely didn't see anything outstanding. I walked up and down four aisles and was about to ask a clerk if there was another drug or discount store I hadn't tried. Then I saw it. High up on the shelves above the check-out counters—displayed more for its ability to attract customers than to actually be purchased— at $38.99 a pricey but perfect fire truck. If I'd shopped it earlier maybe I could have saved a few bucks at one of the big chain toy stores, but under the circumstances I took it with a smile.

The next question was to wrap or not to wrap. (Walgreen is a life-saver at nine-thirty on Christmas Eve, but it doesn't offer courtesy gift wrap!) I opted to wrap it. I was beginning to get into my mis-sion. If I'd gone this far I might as well go all the way. I bought a roll of paper, Scotch tape, and a bag of pre-made bows and did my work in the car.

Now I was ready. It was almost ten and I still wasn't sure exactly where Jamal lived. I wasn't even sure of what I would do when I got there. But I felt like I was finally moving in the right direction— maybe I could make things right after all.

I headed south, then west, driven by an adequate but not out-standing sense of direction. I found the parkway that I thought lead to Jamal's street, but that's where my luck ran out. I drove up and down the same strip three or four times and nothing looked familiar. I was going to have to stop and ask.

Now, let's face it—this is the nineties. Christmas Eve or not, driv-ing around in my little Mercedes 190 with a business suit on was an invitation to trouble. If someone didn't plug me at an intersection, they would surely nail me at the local food mart. That's one good reason why I put off asking as long as I did. When I finally pulled into the best-lit gas station/convenience store I could find, I tried to move like a man with a mission. That was probably the beginning of my downfall. I didn't know it then, but two pairs of eyes were trained on me—had been for the last twenty minutes while I wandered up and down the parkway.

The clerk on duty was about as happy to be working Christmas Eve as I was to be lost in his neighborhood. I bought a pack of gum as a peace offering, then asked for directions to 543 Highland. He still didn't seem too happy about my questions, but eventually he came up with the directions. I put the gum in my pocket and wished him a Merry Christmas. He nodded, put the change in his cash register, then looked up and called after me.

"I wouldn't spend long around here after dark."

What could I say? He was right. Absolutely right. I was insane. Certifiable. What had seemed like a perfect beau geste in my office twenty-five stories above street level now seemed like perfect idiocy. I had gone from Christmas iconoclast to Santa Claus martyr. And why? Because I had a contract with some kid I'd never met and a stubborn desire not to repeat a past wrong. The facts were different. Different race, different times, different home—but like me years before, he was waiting for something special. And I was tired of failing when it came to Christmas.

I sped off from the service station, headed for Jamal's house. That was my second mistake. The car parked over by the side of the food mart turned on its lights and followed. I found that out later.

The directions were faultless. In five minutes I was at Jamal's. The place was small—an old shotgun-style frame—but it was clean and, at least, Jamal had a small yard. He also had a single strand of Christmas lights encircling the front door. That was more than I could claim. There weren't any lights on inside. No one was at home. That would make the job easier. I could just leave the package between the screen and the front door. Jamal would have his present, Sister Pat would have her wish that I remain anonymous, and I would have my peace of mind.

I parked the car and looked around. What did I care if anyone was watching? The best thing I could do was stroll up to the front door, knock on it like I belonged, then simply leave the present when no one answered. But not me. Oh no! I stood by my car for a few minutes, wondering if there might be a side or back door where it would be safer to leave the package. The last thing I wanted was for someone else to take it before Jamal returned home. I walked to the right and peeked around the house. No other entrance was visible. I turned around and took a few steps toward the front door, then thought, No, there's probably a back door—I just didn't see it. I turned again and started down a long, dark side walkway.

That's when everything seemed to happen at once. A floodlight hit me from somewhere on the street. A garbled voice told me to do something—stop, halt, put up my hands, or something to that effect. The floodlight threw me off so much that I couldn't think straight. I panicked, running toward the back of the house. Another floodlight caught me from the darkness at the back of the house. I was pinned between the two lights and I froze like a future road kill.

The lights neared me and I heard clearly now, "Hold up your hands, you are under arrest." I took a deep breath and tried to compose myself. I wasn't going to be shot and left to die. It was the police—even if I couldn't see them. Before I knew it, they were reading me my rights. I tried to interrupt and they kept reading until they were through.

"You don't understand," I continued. "I'm delivering a Christmas gift."

One of the cops laughed. "You're here to buy or sell and maybe take . . . but you're not here to give anything away."

"No, you're wrong. That's exactly why I'm here. Some kid lives here. I've got a fire truck for him."

"What's the family's name?"

I couldn't tell him. Sister Pat wouldn't give me a last name. Just Jamal and the address. Now the lack of the family's last name had me in real trouble.

"We're going downtown. Whatever your story is, they'll listen to you. You can even call your attorney . . . I'm sure you've got one."

"Wait a minute. What's the charge?"

"Reckless driving and trespass for starters . . . then resisting arrest . . . you shouldn't have run. I expect you guys to know better than that. We'll search your car when we can get a warrant. We'll take that 'fire truck' too." They both laughed again. "And when we get a warrant to open it up, we'll see what else old Santa might be bringing for Christmas." The humor in the situation—if there had ever been any—was fading.

"Look," I realized they were serious and that I was going to go "downtown"—it all sounded like a bad episode of "Dragnet"—but I thought maybe, if I was just sincere, "you can search me and my car all you want. You won't find anything. I think someone's going to be very sorry for this."

"Yeah, you," the older voice spoke.

"But come on, let me leave the little boy's gift in the front door."

"Take it," the older voice spoke again. The other cop stepped from behind his light and seized the package before I could do anything. There was definitely no use arguing with them. Still, I tried again and failed. The next thing I knew I was in the back seat of a patrol car, handcuffed and humbled, wondering how I was going to get out of this one, trying to remember if I was entitled to my one phone call the minute I got to the jail or whether I had to wait. Who would I call at eleven o'clock on Christmas Eve? No question about it—Cassandra.

The cops herded me over to a counter and shoved a greasy looking receiver at me. I punched in Cassandra's number. It rang a dozen times before the next guy in line started nudging me in the back. I gave up. The next thing I knew I was in an eight-foot by eight-foot jail cell with six guys who looked like they would kill just because it was a holiday. The arresting officer was explicit. I'd be arraigned in less than an hour and I could make bail by Christmas morning—courtesy of the county's humanitarian program.

My hour seemed to last forever. At first I paced back and forth. Then I got angry. I went to a corner and pounded the wall a few times. The jail walls were built for it and all I got was a numb hand. Then I closed my eyes and tried to imagine myself out. Finally I met resignation, sitting on the floor of the detention cell, my knees pressed up against my chest.

When I was finally led downstairs to the night court, I was demoralized. Six hours before I had been a blissfully oblivious actuary/accountant; self-assured, self-centered, selfish—and happily so—a holdover Yuppie from the eighties. Now, infused with the ghost of Christmas past and the spirit of Christmas present, I was about to become a criminal statistic. Not just some DUI arrest—bad enough—but a felony arrest and a conviction in the making. I was tired and defeated. If I had been asked to confess to the last dozen murders in the city, I probably would have complied. I was not coping well at all.

They took me down an elevator with several other prisoners. I hung my head, staring at the shine on my Allen-Edmonds. I didn't want to see the judge—I might know him; he might even be a client. I certainly didn't want to see anyone else in the courtroom. As I understood it, there was a public defender who would stand in on anyone's behalf—whether he was needy enough or not—just because it was Christmas. I would be called to the bench, acknowledge the charges, plead not guilty, and then do whatever was required to make bail. The guard upstairs had assured me that things would move quickly. After the arraignment, I would get a pretrial date.

Pretrial. An image of my career's end flashed before me. Even if someone eventually believed me and the judge found me not guilty or whatever, the embarrassment of being arrested and having a criminal record would be more than the firm could tolerate. I'd get a week or two of severance, an agreed-upon letter of commendation in my personnel file, a day or two to wrap things up with what had once been my clients, then I'd be gone. I would be ruined. All over a fire truck for some poor kid named Jamal.

I heard my name called. I lurched forward, eyes on the floor, feeling like I was in a very bad Kafka novel. But before I could distance myself from anything less than a plea of not guilty, I heard my first name spoken by a female voice. I looked up from my place behind a huge mountain of tatoos—a pleasant fellow charged with beating his brother's wife with their Christmas tree—and peeked meekly around him.

"Cassandra?" It was her all right. Ready to prosecute to the limits of the law in a moment's notice.

"You know this prisoner?" The judge emitted a noncommittal monotone. To personally know anyone being arraigned must be bad for one's career.

"I do, Your Honor. Could I have one moment with him before the arraignment?"

The judge nodded and so did my would-be counsel from the public defender's office. Then they both looked at each other and shrugged. The whole slew of them—Cassandra included—should have been nominated for sainthood for doing duty on Christmas Eve. But I also knew they'd want to get out of there as soon as possible, and, as confirmation, the judge, the public defender, and the skeleton crew of court personnel immediately trained their eyes on the clock. Whatever Cassandra and I said to each other would have to be brief.

"What are you doing here?" Cassandra asked as she read down the indictment.

I spoke as quickly as I could. I skipped all the details but I started out with our last date, the slip of paper, how I discovered it in my suit pocket, the investigation that lead to Jamal and his address, buying the fire truck, wrapping it up, getting lost, finding Jamal's house, and then getting arrested. When I was finished, Cassandra must have realized that my tale was too ridiculous to be a lie. She simply shook her head, then told me to stand where I was.

She walked to the judge's bench. The public defender joined her. I couldn't hear a thing they said, but whatever she told them it took half as long as I had taken with Cassandra. There was some back and forth, a few nods of the head, then the judge looked up and cleared his throat.

He addressed me formally, then paused. "The county attorney has just told me your story. I've been on the district court for twelve years and I've heard some incredible tales in that time—but yours takes top honors! But then Christmas always seems to bring out the kooks. I am accepting the county attorney's word as an officer of the court, and, as such, dismissing all charges and releasing you to go home." Short and sweet, he brought the gavel down.

There was an immediate roar of applause and favorable mumbles from prisoners and court personnel alike. The judge brought his gavel down again.

"If you'll take this note down to the property room," he scribbled something quickly and gave it to the court bailiff to give to me, "they'll give you your fire truck back." The courtroom broke out in laughter and I turned redder than the fire truck itself.

Cassandra came back to me as the judge called the next case. "I'll be through these arraignments in twenty minutes." She paused, looked away, and smiled. Then she turned back to me. "If you wait for me, I can get us a police escort back to Jamal's."

For the first time all night I felt as if Christmas had finally arrived. This was a lot better than an arrest record.

"It's a date," I said.

As a matter of fact, it turned out to be the best date we ever had. From the time that Cassandra met me downstairs, Jamal's fire truck tucked safely under my arm, until the last goodnight kiss we exchanged well after midnight on Christmas morning, I was totally possessed by the spirit of Christmas. It even continued into the next week when Sister Pat called to report that Jamal had been most astounded to find that there was indeed a Santa Claus. How else would that fabulous fire truck have presented itself so long after he and his family had gotten home from church that Christmas Eve? How indeed?

St. Nicholas
of the Neighborhood

St. Nicholas of the Neighborhood

THIS ISN'T ONE OF THOSE saccharine Christmas stories. This is no peaceful, Christmas-Eve-in-the-suburbs sort of tale. We don't even live in a suburb! I wish we did! Life would be easier. This is a Christmas tragedy. It's full of pathos and violence and parental abuse and even bared skin—this is a hard, tough Christmas carol (how's that for a come-on?) for everybody who is tired of those kiddie Christmas stories!

It began on a peaceful, Christmas Eve morning while I was brushing my teeth. Christmas Eve fell on a Sunday that year, so I was also headed for church. I wasn't headed there too quickly. In fact, I was feeling lucky to be way ahead of schedule. The early service wasn't for another two hours, and for some reason I had gotten up early. Early and feeling half human at that. There was going to be time for a cup of coffee, the Sunday paper, and maybe even a little Charles Kuralt—back before even that joy disappeared. Life was good!

Tad was still young enough to be in the church Christmas pageant, even if he didn't want to be, and Molly was going to be the baby Jesus. (At her age even Hollywood doesn't distinguish between boys and girls.) I was supposed to open the service with a men's chorus—I might not like it, but I could stand it. My wife was directing the whole shebang. Wife, son, and daughter were already

149

at church chafing over the production details and I was all alone in my peace on earth. I was standing there, brushing my teeth, not looking much like St. Nicholas. I hadn't shaved or showered or combed my hair, which was standing sideways and on end like a very bad toupee. But why worry? I had all the time in the world. Typical, kiss of death, muse.

The phone rang. I ignored it. I was resolved to preserve my Sunday solitude. Besides, no one worth talking to would call at 8:00 A.M. on Sunday morning. It rang again. What if it was my wife? What if they were in trouble? What if there had been a death in the family? One more, irritating ring. Nothing melts resolve quicker than a third ring of the phone.

I spat out the foam, and with mouth tingling, sparkling, and brighter than any out of a Pepsodent commercial, I raced for our bedroom and the nearest phone. A fourth ring and it would bounce over into the recorder's "Hello, we are not at home right now, but if you'll leave your message at the sound of the tone . . ." over which I had no control since I was upstairs and it was in the kitchen. I grabbed the phone.

"Hello . . ." Too late. The recording had begun and I had to listen to my wife's well-modulated voice politely telling the burglars waiting across the street that we weren't at home. (No, there weren't burglars across the street but I always imagined that they were the callers who hung up before the phone beeped.) In the distance I could hear a woman's voice trying to speak over the message.

"Whoever's there . . . hang on," I said. "We're upstairs. At least I'm upstairs. I can't hear you now, but if you'll wait until the recording's done, I'll be here." I felt a little stupid, but electronic gizmos always make me feel stupid, so it was nothing new.

"I can't believe I caught you!" I knew by her voice that it was Sandy Payne, our neighbor three blocks down the street.

"Hey, what's up? I thought you all were going to be in Florida for the holidays."

"We are in Florida. That's the problem."

"Doesn't sound like much of a problem to me!" I am often capable of witty repartee such as this at 8:00 A.M. and generally my friends are more tolerant than Sandy was at that moment.

"Look, this is important . . ." [stupid] "I need to ask a big favor. I mean really big. This could be the biggest favor ever. I mean it. I wouldn't ask if you all weren't such good friends. I'm going to owe you . . ."

"Okay. Okay. Small denominations—unmarked bills—would be nice. Now what will you owe me for?"

"Okay. So we're in Florida . . . " I looked out the window on a sheet of ice spreading like a glacier.

"Don't remind me," I interrupted.

"Okay, you're not going to believe this, but all of Matt's Santa Claus presents are back home at Loretta's." Loretta was Matt's grandmother.

"Well, how did that happen?" I asked incisively.

A steely edge invaded Sandy's honey-perfect Southern accent. "Skip and I haven't quite . . . figured . . . that . . . one . . . out . . . yet . . ."

"Now don't blame me for it!" I could hear Skip's voice in the background pleading his innocence. I knew already that, guilty or not, it was his burden to bear.

"And who am I going to blame? You didn't pick them up at Loretta's!" Sandy had covered the receiver with the palm of her hand, but everyone knows that only works in movies.

"And you didn't remind me! You were outside in the car waiting!"

"Sandy! Sandy!" I shouted. "Forget how it happened!"

Her voice back on the phone, controlled, well-modulated. Ah, Southern women! "Still there? I'm sorry. I had to ask Skip something. Well, we're in a fix. All of Matt's toys are at Loretta's."

"So you want me to help Loretta get them to you?" I could tell by the long silence that I had asked another bad question.

"Loretta is already here . . . with us!" Sandy's voice shot up and I could tell she was losing it. "You can see where I'm going with this, can't you?"

"Well, yes and no. I mean, it's Christmas Eve and unless you know something I don't, Santa comes this evening. Am I right so far?"

"Here's the plan . . ." I love Southern women. They are always in control even when circumstances would suggest they aren't. ". . . you need to go to our house, crawl through the basement window . . ."

"Now hold on. I'll get caught and put in jail!"

"No you won't! As soon as we get off the phone I'll call the next-door neighbors. It'll be okay. They're very old or I would ask Mr. Carver to do this himself."

"You are desperate." I was feeling older by the moment—but not old enough to beg out of this task of friendship.

"You're right, I'm desperate. Matt's Christmas is over at Loretta's!"

"Okay. Okay." Anything to quell the rising hysteria in her voice.

"You go into the house, turn off the alarm before it alerts the alarm company . . ."

"Where's the alarm?"

"In the kitchen, you can't miss it. You de-program the alarm—

punch in 01982—pick up the keys to Loretta's apartment—also in the kitchen—go over there . . ."

"And how do I leave your house?"

"Well . . ." She had to think. Evidently the general's plans had one or two minor flaws. ". . . best bet is to leave by the front door—there's a dead bolt—our front door key is right under Loretta's on the hook in the kitchen."

"Can't I keep it, just in case I decide to come back for the TV and the VCR?"

"Very funny. Then you go to Loretta's apartment. Her key works in the third lock from the bottom . . . or is it the second? Well, anyway, there's two locks. You'll have about five or six keys. You should be able to figure it out. Once you get inside, call me."

"Is that so if I don't call, you'll know the Carvers have turned me over to the police?"

"Just call me. I'm not sure where the presents are and I'll describe them to you."

"Sandy, is this some sort of television show you're doing? Sort of a world's funniest friends on Christmas Eve or something? You know, catch the old dad doing something really dumb and then video him?"

"Look, they're in bags and Loretta has lots of bags around. Just call me."

"Okay, then what?"

"There's a nine-thirty flight to Tampa. Get it to the airport before then, they'll put the presents in a box, and we'll have them by mid-afternoon. Miss it, and you've missed the last flight before the evening, and that will be too late."

I looked at my watch. It was eight-oh-five. "Nine-thirty is no problem," I chuckled. "Because I have to be back here, showered, shaved, and dressed to sing by nine-fifteen."

"Perfect."

"Yeah, perfect, but I've got to throw on some jeans and leave now."

"You're a saint." Sandy's commando control voice softened. "You're a real, honest-to-God saint."

"Please, Sandy. The original deal was for a big check or maybe even cash."

"Don't make light, it's unbecoming a saint. Now here's the number. Call me at Loretta's." She wound up the details, gave me her number and the neighbor's first names, repeated the secret code for the burglar alarm, told me to take in cash for the air parcel, and then sprinkled around a few minor details. I hung up and realized my coffee had grown cold. So much for early mornings. Next time I'll sleep later.

I parked in front of the Paynes' house feeling like some second-story man casing the joint. I looked at the Carvers' house on the right. It was dark. Not a sign of human life. The house on the left was the same. They were all waiting for me. I knew it. One move for the house and they'd be on their phones. It was very early on a Sunday, Christmas Eve morning. I was unshaven, in jeans and sneakers with an old Oertel's 92 beer cap on to cover my greasy hair, and my twenty-year-old football jacket snapped up tight to my neck. Nothing suspicious. No. Not much.

I got out of the car and tried not to look around. I immediately failed miserably, gaping in every possible direction to see if anyone was watching. My breath formed giant white clouds. I hadn't checked the thermometer or listened to the radio but it had to be in the teens. I should have been back in bed dreaming of sugar plums. But no, here I was in a neighborhood where everyone knew everyone else and were all probably looking out their windows at the drifter staring aimlessly at their homes. I felt like a goldfish.

I started up the front stairs and someone passed in a car and waved. I waved back. Oh no, I thought, they think I'm Skip. But now they've seen my face and they know I'm not Skip. They know Skip's out of town. They know Skip isn't expecting anyone. They know that anyone skulking around Skip's house must be a prowler, maybe even a burglar. Great! Move along. Stay cool. Don't look suspicious.

With the last thought I started two steps at a time up the steep front stairs. Dummy. I should have known. The walks were a sheet of ice. My feet flew up and I grabbed for the wrought iron rail to my side. My face was only an inch from the top step when I caught my fall. What a beginning!

When I looked up, an old man was standing at the top of the steps. He was wearing green trousers, a red sweater, and a white shirt. He was definitely amused. I couldn't blame him.

"You must be Sandy and Skip's friend?" His face rose upward in a friendly mass of wrinkles.

"You must be Mr. Carver."

"My friends call me Puck."

"Sidewalks are a little slick," I groaned, rising to my knees, then my feet.

"If you're not careful," he chuckled.

Nice guy. I'm practically knocked out of action in the first round and Puck is telling me I ought to be more careful.

"You know why I'm here?"

"Sure. Follow me."

Walking less steadily than my octogenarian guide, I followed him to the side window, my supposed portal to the house. Fat chance! I took one look and shook my head. This was no window. It was actually an old coal chute and it looked about as big as a dryer vent. My old football player's hips and shoulders weren't going to squeeze through. No wonder Sandy and Skip left it unlocked. Only a mouse burglar would offer a threat.

"You want me to try?" Puck had noticed my disbelief. Now he was trying to shame me.

"No, I'll do it. Just give me a second to get small."

"I'll prop it open with this broom." Puck was at least a man of action.

I got down on my belly and slithered backwards until my feet touched glass. Puck pushed with his broom, the window swung from top hinges inward, and I blindly inched into the darkness. My hips went through, then my waist, and I was trying to slide down the rest of the way when I stopped. Like a human teeter-totter I tilted first toward the black abyss of the Paynes' basement, then toward the brown dirt and leaves that were about an inch from my face.

"You're doing fine." Puck spurred me on. Easy for him to say. "Keep it up, son," he urged. Ah, the fatherly touch . . .

"Whoaaaa!" I teetered or tottered too far and dissolved into the darkness of the Paynes' basement. Actually it was more like a cellar—or a dungeon. I immediately imagined a thousand spiders plunking their webs in anticipation of Christmas dinner—me. I hadn't brought a flashlight and I couldn't find a light switch, but in a few seconds my eyes grew accustomed to the dark and the light from the coal chute was enough to see steps.

"Are you okay down there?" Good old Puck seemed miles away.

"I think so."

"Don't forget the alarm." He paused and I knew he was chuckling again. "You've got about a minute left."

The alarm! I had to get up the stairs, find the number panel to the alarm, and punch in the "kill" code. I ran for the steps and promptly stubbed my toe, tripped on the bottom step, and slammed my left shin. In the dark I could feel the skin on my right palm scraped from top to bottom. (That's where the bared skin part of this story comes in.) There was no time to think about it. I rushed upstairs, went to the kitchen, and looked inside the pantry. There it was—the control panel. Thirty seconds left.

It was 1963 again. James Bond. *Goldfinger.* Miss the code and the cops would be all over me. I punched it in: 19820. I waited, smug and satisfied. Twenty-five seconds left—twenty-four—twenty-three.

"Come on!" I cried out. What had Sandy said if not 19820?

Twenty-two—twenty-one—twenty. The seconds were ticking. Why had I answered the phone? Why did I let Sandy talk me into this? Yes, she was my son's friend's mother. Yes, she was charming and attractive. Yes, I am just a weak, white American male—the target of every political interest group in America today and a sucker for a woman's charm—but why me? What was the combination? 01982? It had something to do with 1982? It was worth a try. I started and messed up. A clumsy white American man at that. My hands were sweating. I tried again. Ten—nine—eight—seven. Five more seconds and the neighborhood would really get a show. I punched in 01982. The beeping stopped. A miracle. Not a holy miracle or a Christmas miracle or even a minor miracle. Probably it was just dumb luck. But it stopped.

I checked my watch. Eight-twenty. I was in trouble. I had to move fast. I looked for the keys. They were on the hook, just where they were supposed to be. I grabbed them, or grabbed at them. Then hook, key ring, keys—everything—came off the wall and dispersed across the kitchen floor. Not only that, I hadn't the faintest idea which one unlocked Sandy and Skip's front door.

I swept them all into my bleeding palm and started picking and fumbling through them while I walked to the front door. I chose one that looked like a key to a dead bolt and tried it in the cylinder. No good. By now Puck had come around to the front. He was standing in front of me on the porch, waving. I grinned and did my best. He diligently watched me choose one, then another. No good. I tried again. That was when I realized he was trying to tell me which key was the right one. I held up the remaining keys one by one. Like charades. He waved "no" or "hold it up to the light" and finally "yes."

I opened the door. "How did you know?"

"I used to be a locksmith," he announced with supreme non-chalance.

"You mean you could have gotten me in the front door?"

"Sure, I suppose so," he said.

"Why didn't you!"

"Sandy said 'through the basement window' and it *is* her house."

"But it's my flesh and blood," and I held up my palm, only now beginning to throb a little.

"I thought you were going to be younger—more agile." It was the first time all morning that he didn't crack a smile.

"I give up!"

"Not now you don't. Your job is only half done!" He was grinning again. "And without the Christmas presents, half isn't worth anything at all."

"You're right." What else could I say? I threw the remaining keys in my right pocket, activated the alarm, re-locked the front door, gave the key to Puck, and made good my escape. Eight-twenty-five. It had been less than a half hour, but it felt like a week.

"Good luck, son," Puck called after me as I hobbled down the front steps.

"I'll be back for some eggnog," I called back.

Loretta's carriage house apartment was only two blocks away. I parked in the alley, jumped out of the car, and in seconds was doing my key routine again. A voice from behind told me that my next assistant was no Puck Carver.

"Hey, you. What are you doing?"

I've come to steal little Matthew's Christmas presents. That's why I'm standing here in my jeans, a two-day growth, a beaten-up jock jacket, and a hand wrapped in a bloody handkerchief. Any more questions, ace? Of course I didn't have the nerve to say it. Good thing.

I turned around. "I'm a friend of Loretta's son. They're all in Florida. They left their presents behind by mistake. I've got to take them to the airport." This was definitely no genial neighbor. This fellow looked only slightly better than I felt. His grizzle was permanent and the sneer on his face wasn't for the benefit of the serial killer whom he had trapped in front of Loretta's carriage house.

"Show me some identification."

"Okay, here's my wallet." I reached behind me. He backed away. I suddenly realized this guy had a gun. Christmas flashed before my eyes. Christmas without old Dad.

"Look," I said as politely as my cracking voice would permit, "put that down." I turned around so that my back faced him, then got my wallet out of my hip pocket. "Look all you want," I said as he took my wallet, "but I've got to try to find a key that will work in this door. Okay?"

"Okay, but don't try anything funny."

"Fine." I had, in my nervousness, some sarcasm I wanted to share about his Sgt. Joe Friday tone and mannerism, but I wisely held my tongue. I started working at the keys. On try three it worked. I was getting better.

"Well, this all looks in order," my neighborhood vigilante friend observed, "but I don't know."

"Why don't you just come in with me?"

This caught him off guard. I was inviting him to become an accessory to breaking and entering. Well, actually I hadn't broken anything, but he probably sensed I was up to no good. He hesitated.

"Come on," I urged. "I'm going in. Then I'm going to find the presents. Then I'm going to call Sandy Payne. You can talk to Loretta. I presume you all know each other. Then I've got ten minutes to get to the airport. Okay?" Down boy. Nice boy.

"I'll go in. But . . ."

"I won't try anything funny," I interrupted.

I swung Loretta's front door inward and flipped on the lights. I checked my watch. Eight-thirty. With my guardian angel at my rear I went upstairs and found the first phone.

"I'm going to call the Paynes now." I felt like I was defusing a bomb. I punched in their number.

"Hello." Sandy's voice, still strained, almost tearful this time.

"Sandy, the eagle has landed."

"Oh, thank God! Did everything go okay?"

"Later. For now, could you just get Loretta on the phone. I've got a friend of hers who wants to talk to her for a second."

I put the long arm of the neighborhood's law on the phone and watched his face soften as he talked to Loretta. They spoke for a second and when it was clear that I could reassume my air of high-handed moral indignation without getting my head blown off I motioned for him to return the receiver. He complied.

"Loretta, let me talk to Sandy one more time."

A second later Sandy was on the phone. I was smiling pleasantly at the neighbor. Cupping my hand over the receiver I said as subtly as possible, "You can go now." He nodded, said no more, and left.

"Are you still there?" Sandy's voice on the other end.

"Yes, I'm here. Luckily, bright eyes just left."

"You were lucky he didn't shoot you. He's a gun nut and a real law-and-order kind of guy."

"Now you tell me!"

"I forgot." Sandy had shifted into her mellow-as-fine-bourbon voice.

"Okay, well, what's next?"

"Look around for a green and gold striped bag—actually three bags." I looked around as she spoke.

"I don't see them."

"Look in Loretta's bedroom."

I put the phone down and followed orders. No bags. Nowhere. While I was at it, I looked in closets and behind doors, even under the bed. Nothing. No green and gold striped bags anywhere.

"Sandy," my voice must have shown my defeat, "I can't find a thing. And it's not as if this apartment is all that big."

"Let me think. Let me think." Her voice was frantic, strained.

"I'll look in the kitchen and the living room."

I looked, but it didn't do any good. Maybe I hadn't been the first intruder in Loretta's apartment that Christmas Eve morning. I looked again in every possible corner. Time was running out . . . for the flight to Tampa, for my Sunday morning service, for Matt's Christmas.

"Sandy, have you thought of anything? They're just not here."

Silence. A long sigh. A quiet pursing of lips. A slight sniffle. "I can't think of a thing."

"I hate to say it," I said. "But I've got to get going."

"Okay. I understand."

We hung up and I stood there for a second. Now I was frustrated. Frustrated and mad. I had given up the morning, half the skin on my palm, and more than a little mental energy trying to play St. Nicholas. For what? I sat down on the end of Loretta's bed and set my jaw. This wouldn't do. I thought through the scene of Sandy, Skip, Loretta, and Matt leaving for the airport.

"Got everything?"

"Yes."

"Turn off the lights."

"Okay."

"Grab the suitcases."

"Okay."

"Take them to the car, I'll be right there."

"Where's the car?"

Then it came to me. The car would be in the back! Skip would have taken the suitcases out the back, not the front. The back of the carriage house was on the alley, and on the back there was an enclosed porch and stairs.

I rushed to the kitchen and the back door, threw it open, and there they were. Three green and gold striped bags! I smiled, then laughed. If only Sandy and Skip had remembered, I would have never had to break into the Paynes', prevent the burglar alarm from going off, struggle with the keys, meet Rex the wonder neighbor, and get very late for the pageant service. I would have simply driven to Loretta's, gone up her back stairs, and headed off for the airport. This is the pathos part.

Enough pathos, I told myself. Time for action. I turned off the lights, locked up, and moved the bags to my car. I glanced at my watch. Eight-forty. The nine-thirty service was looking iffy.

The airport wasn't far away—a fact we are reminded of every night between 11:00 P.M. and 1:00 A.M.—and traffic on a Sunday, Christmas Eve morning was less than teeming, though the traffic I encountered moved like cold glue. I probably scared some folks with my driving and some of the things I muttered probably weren't very Christian as I reflect back on it, but I got there in ten minutes. After that I wasn't taking any chances. I parked right in front of the Delta Departures sign, told the airport police that I was on a mission of mercy (which they quickly surmised as I grabbed up the three green and gold bags), and raced for the Delta counter.

"Gotta get these on the nine-thirty flight for Tampa!" I shouted.

"Merry Christmas!" the tired-looking woman rejoined.

"Will I make it?"

Airlines employees are always unflappable in these situations. It must be part of their training. She gently took my wrist, smiled, and said simply: "I'll make sure of it." She picked up the phone, called the gate, and told whoever was there to hold for one second. Then she threw the bags in a big box, sealed it up, wrote PAYNE in big letters per my instructions, and called another employee who came and whisked it away. Gone. Out of my hands. Out of my control.

"Were they your family's or someone else's?" she asked now that we had a moment to breathe.

"Friends'. They forgot their son's Christmas presents."

"And you went and got them for them."

"Yeah, I guess so."

"Well, Merry Christmas, my friend. You're okay." She paused. "That will be $21.50."

"Well worth it," I said.

"Funny the things we do this time of year."

"Yeah," I said. "Don't tell me there isn't a spirit of Christmas. Though it does hurt sometimes." I held up my hand, the handkerchief now dirty as well as crusty red.

"Ouch!" she cried out in sympathy. "You better get home and take care of that."

Home! In the brief lull I had forgotten all about my own family, Tad, Molly, and my wife's Christmas pageant, the church service in which I was supposed to anchor the baritones in the men's chorus. They had no idea where I was, what I had been doing, or why I had done it. I looked at my watch. Nine-ten. Impossible. I couldn't make it.

"Thanks." I took her hand with my good hand. "I'm late!"

With that I made my exit. No longer were the angels on my side. If there was a slow-moving vehicle within a mile, it gravitated immediately to me. The trip that took me ten minutes going took me almost twenty minutes coming back. At nine-thirty-five I approached my own house and debated the alternatives. They were simple. Go home, shower, look human, and miss the service, or put a sack over my head and skulk into the back of the sanctuary looking like Freddie the Freeloader. Minus the bag, I chose the second course of action.

As I tiptoed up the side steps of the church I could hear the strains of the men's chorus—only slightly weakened by my absence—sounding forth the final verse of our Christmas carol. Oh well, I thought, maybe next year. I opened the door. It squeaked. There, staring me in the eyes were my family. My wife, with "script" in hand, Tad, a reluctant shepherd, and Molly, wrapped in swaddling and soundly asleep. They were surrounded by the requisite number of angels and archangels, assistant shepherds, and, of course, Mary. My wife never missed a beat. (This is where the parental abuse comes in.)

"I thought you were in the shower . . ." she whispered. "I'm glad you saw the message beeping on the telephone. Thanks for not shaving. Adds a great touch. You look great! Perfect!"

And with that she threw some old burlap around my shoulders, took off my Oertel's 92 hat, and wrapped some striped cloth around my head before I could say "how do you do" or "Merry Christmas." The organ started playing, the choir and congregation struck up "The First Noel," and my wife positioned me next to Mary. At that moment Jesus awoke, looked at me contentedly, and went back to sleep.

Dad. Good old work-at-the-carpentry-shop-every-day Dad! Yes, unwittingly, unknowingly, and with no exercise of free will on my part, I had been transformed into Joseph—the ultimate stepparent! I found out later that the first-string Joseph had come down with a twenty-four-hour virus and I was the miraculous answer to my wife's call to central casting. (Thus are legends made.)

"Just walk slowly, look devout, and turn slightly to the left when you get to the front. Mary will show you the rest," my wife whispered in my ear. "Hope you had a peaceful morning at home," she added as she kissed my stubbly cheek.

I made it down the aisle half-dazed. Friends told me later it was the perfect touch. The pageant went off without a hitch, and, like old Joseph, I was the perfect straight man. Baby Jesus never even whimpered.

And so the story ends. Blood, violence, pathos, and parental abuse. All the makings of a morning with a talk show host! I love this country, I love Christmas, and I love my family! But the next time the phone rings on a Sunday morning, Christmas Eve, somebody else is answering it!